# TEEN GIRL'S HANDBOOK

*From Making Friends, Avoiding Drama,
Overcoming Insecurities, Planning for
the Future, and Everything Else Along
the Way to Growing Up*

By

**KAREN HARRIS**

# FREE BONUS

## SCAN TO GET OUR NEXT BOOK FOR FREE!

# Table of Contents

# INTRODUCTION

Welcome to the unique world of being a teen girl! This handbook is designed to provide you with information and guidance along your path through teenage girlhood. The goal is for you to have a basic reference book to help address and navigate common subjects and issues that are frequently faced by girls within this wide age group of 13 through 19. This includes body changes, setting boundaries, developing leadership skills, dating, responsible use of social media, and overall management of your physical, mental, and emotional health, among many other things. Certain topics related to your growth and development as a teen girl may be difficult for you to discuss with family members, friends, or even medical professionals, depending on your cultural background, previous experiences, and levels of anxiety or shyness. This handbook can answer some of your questions, but even more importantly, it can give you the encouragement and confidence to advocate for yourself and seek advice and support when you need it.

Some sections of this handbook may not apply to you directly during specific points on the timeline of your teenage years. For example, it's unlikely that you would be as concerned about or interested in financial independence, work experience, or internships at 14 as you would be at 18. However, each topic is here for you to reference and consult when you need it. In addition, reading and re-reading throughout these pages is a great strategy to help you prepare for what's to come or process what you've learned and how far you've progressed. In other words, you can approach this handbook as something to read from cover to cover, or you can choose to read just the chapters and sections that relate to your current experience and then return to it throughout your journey as a teenager.

Of course, it would be impossible to present a comprehensive manual that addresses everything about being a teen girl or covers how to handle all situations. That's why it's important to consider this book as a general guide with practical information and ideas, as well as supportive and inspirational content. Some approaches and/or strategies may not apply directly to your specific situations, yet the advice in this handbook can provide you with a foundation for navigating the teenage years in general. You may even be inspired to do further research or read about a potential career, educational path, or movement to support, in addition to learning about important and impactful women of the past and present.

Ultimately, your experiences, personality, and talents are uniquely yours, regardless of your age, and they will blossom and grow as you mature. You have the capability as a young woman to make your future dreams come true — no matter what they are — through education and learning, developing life skills and experience, and nurturing your relationship with yourself and others. And someday, you may have the opportunity to positively impact and inspire other teen girls. So, let's get started on your teen girl journey of discovery, empowerment, and fun!

# CHAPTER ONE:
# THE JOURNEY OF
# SELF-DISCOVERY

The teen years are unlike any other stage of life. Between 13 and 19 years old, girls typically navigate the transitions from middle school to high school to college and/or the start of a career, with significant physical and emotional changes, shifting dynamics in relationships, and expanding personal values and worldviews. On top of these dramatic developments, teen girls must manage their health, time, and plans for the future. This journey from girlhood to womanhood in just over half a decade can certainly appear overwhelming. However, it's also a journey of self-discovery that can set you on the path to a lifetime of success and personal fulfillment.

Though every generation of teenagers has its own struggles, culture, and defining moments, being a teen girl at this point in time comes with significantly different pressures, opportunities, and experiences. Many current teens consider themselves global citizens, with unprecedented awareness and concern regarding environmental, social, and political issues. Technology allows for greater access to information than ever yet must be balanced with the risk of exposure to distressing situations and complex data that even adults can't comprehend. Teenagers are expanding the definitions of identity and diversity while facing drastic changes in terms of academic structure, socialization, and even safety. All these elements are in addition to the pressures to succeed, make life-changing decisions, and become self-reliant.

Yet one thing remains pretty much the same in terms of going through the teen years. It is a journey of growth and discovery. As a teen girl, you will learn as much about yourself as you will about the world around you. This includes your interests, passions, talents, strengths, and many other qualities that make up the individual that you are. You will also impact others through your relationships and friendships and all the activities in which you participate. Along this journey, you can expect to develop wisdom, make mistakes, achieve some goals, laugh, cry, build resilience, and undergo almost anything else that falls within the human condition and experience.

Thankfully, the highs and lows of your self-discovery during the teenage years will help you prepare and move toward adulthood. You'll have a better understanding of what you'd like to pursue for your future, whether that involves higher education, a specific career track, travel, hobbies, or other goals. In addition, you'll have developed compassion, generosity, and empathy toward others that will help you make a difference in the world. You'll have learned to forgive yourself and others for mistakes, as well as how to persevere in the face of setbacks.

Of course, by the time you reach your 20th birthday, the official end of being a teenager, you'll still have numerous opportunities to grow, learn, and discover even more about yourself as an adult. Yet you'll have a strong and hard-won foundation of learning and experience as a basis for building the rest of your life due to your teenage journey.

# UNDERSTANDING YOUR EVOLVING IDENTITY

Your identity is made up of your personality, character traits, beliefs, and manner of expression. Identity is a dynamic concept of "self" that we develop beginning in childhood, and it is constantly undergoing change. In fact, humans are almost always a work in progress in terms of who they are, regardless of age, life situation, and other factors. This is largely because we are impacted by our experiences, world events, relationships, learning, and more, all of which shift our individual perspectives and conceptualizations of ourselves.

It's important to understand, therefore, that your identity will continue to evolve throughout your teenage years. Just as you wouldn't expect yourself to be the exact same person at 13 as you were at 10, you will be a different form of yourself at 18 than you are at 13, and so forth. It can seem intimidating at first to think of undergoing such significant changes, but the concept of your identity evolving can actually be rather comforting. It means that you are growing as an individual, broadening your perspective and understanding, and gaining wisdom. These changes will provide you with greater opportunities and new experiences in addition to supporting your increased independence.

Of course, time, maturity, and age play significant roles in the way our identities evolve. This is especially true in the teen years as your body and brain grow and develop. However, your identity isn't solely based on your age, grade in school, hometown, or any other outward characteristics or demographics. In fact, the concept of identity is often much more a reflection of our inner perceptions, beliefs, and feelings. Part of our human nature is to apply labels to ourselves and others. For example, you may describe your best friend as funny, interesting, supportive, and athletic. And your best friend may describe you as intelligent, kind, quirky, and honest. Though these labels are likely to be true, they certainly wouldn't be comprehensive in describing the full identities of either you or your best friend — and they may even differ from how you would describe yourselves.

With that in mind, as you discover and understand your evolving identity, it's beneficial to remember that there are almost limitless ways to define and describe who you are. Your core values and relationships will probably remain about the same, but you will have many opportunities to expand your view of the world and how you fit into it. In addition, the more you learn and experience, the more your internal perceptions, beliefs, and feelings are likely to evolve and progress. This allows you to grow and mature as well as see yourself in a different light.

As your identity evolves during your teen years, it's also important to be patient with yourself and others. You can expect to feel indecision, frustration, and confusion at times in terms of how you see yourself compared to how others might view you, especially family members who have known you all your life. This is especially true as you grow more independent and want to take on greater responsibilities, which may conflict with other people's perceptions of your strengths and abilities. You may have the self-confidence to do certain things on your own, but face restrictions put in place by your parents or society. For example, you may feel ready for an after-school job at 15 but find that many places have an age minimum of 16 for hiring. In this case, you can take the opportunity to find a volunteer job rather than a paid position or patiently wait until your next birthday while pursuing other activities in the meantime. As long as you are able to move forward and remain resilient, your identity will continue to evolve and actualize in a positive way.

Overall, your identity is made up of combinations of almost infinite external and internal factors. As you evolve as a person, your identity will do the same. Understanding and embracing all the qualities of your "self," as well as your continued growth and development, will give you the confidence and courage to be and become the best version of yourself in your teen years and beyond.

# OVERCOMING INSECURITIES

Two of the most important parts of your self-discovery journey are overcoming your insecurities and embracing self-love. These are some of the most challenging aspects of the teen years (and beyond) for many people and can be an even greater struggle for girls. In fact, statistics show that there is a noticeable drop in self-esteem and well-being reported by adolescent girls as early as ages 11–12. Lower self-esteem in teen girls can be attributed to many factors, including issues with body image, poor performance in school, stressful home environment, mental health difficulties, and other insecurities. Diminished well-being is likely a result of not only lower self-esteem but also unhealthy habits and behavior patterns, excessive screen time, and inadequate self-care.

At a young age, girls, in particular, receive both implicit and overt messages that somehow they don't measure up to society's "standards." This can create insecurities related to appearance, intelligence, popularity, personality, athleticism, and even family income. Unfortunately, social media, advertising, and celebrity culture all work to compound this issue by presenting an often unrealistic portrayal of the way people are living their lives and distorted images of how people actually look. Even individuals with the strongest sense of self can feel inadequate against the bombardment of professional marketing campaigns, "influencer" posts, and other pervasive impressions of the "perfect" face, hair, body, social life, career, etc. Though you may recognize at an intellectual level that there is no such thing as perfection, it can be hard to resist judging our differences as imperfections.

The truth is that everyone faces insecurities about themselves because that's just human nature. Therefore, the goal in overcoming insecurities is to frame them properly — and this is a pattern of thinking that can be difficult to embrace at first because it involves a commitment to mindful thinking. Essentially, most of our insecurities come from our own thoughts and not from measurable facts. For example, height is measurable. You can compare yourself to someone and factually know in that moment if you are taller or shorter. Though you may wish to be a different height, there's no point in dwelling on that insecurity because it's beyond your control. On the other hand, something like popularity is nearly impossible to measure. You may compare yourself to someone else at school who seems to have more friends, self-confidence, and social presence. However, these are not facts. They are thoughts that come from internal assumptions and impressions. Understanding this can help you frame any insecurities about your popularity or someone else's. Since they don't come from measurable facts, these insecurities are basically unfounded, and it would be a waste of time and energy to dwell on them.

Teen girls tend to spend a lot of time internally comparing themselves to others, whether their peers or public figures. Unfortunately, this can bring about an overload of insecure thoughts and feelings centered around physical appearance, accomplishments, likability, and more. However, training your brain to be mindful and avoid comparisons is the key to overcoming this negative pattern. There are many ways to do this, but it takes purposeful effort. Here are some suggestions to help you overcome thoughts of insecurity:

- Make a list that separates measurable facts from your internal thoughts and assumptions.
- Keep a journal of your insecure feelings but also positive self-affirmations that include your wonderful qualities and personal achievements.
- Strictly limit your time online and with social media. Replace it with other activities such as reading, exercise, volunteering, music, learning something new, or other things you enjoy.
- Practice gratitude every day for nature, health, family, friends, abilities, freedoms, and more.

- Remind yourself to be happy for the successes and achievements of others because they don't diminish your own in the slightest.
- Embrace self-love.

Some people misunderstand the concept of self-love, confusing it with a form of arrogance or narcissism. In truth, self-love equals gratitude plus self-care. Loving and being grateful for who you are is not only healthy, but it strengthens your self-esteem and self-worth. Caring for yourself is also essential and an important part of growth and maturity as a teen girl. This includes practicing physical self-care in the form of healthy eating, exercise, and adequate sleep, but it also involves caring for yourself emotionally and mentally. Make sure that you balance work and fun as much as possible, be kind and forgiving toward yourself, and reach out for support when you need it.

# FINDING YOUR VOICE AND PERSONAL STYLE

One of the best and most fun aspects of your self-discovery journey is finding your voice and personal style. You are completely unique as an individual, and the way you express yourself internally and externally should reflect that. Sometimes, as a teenager, it's difficult to find the self-confidence to stand out or be different from your peers, especially in terms of your image or personal passions. However, it's far more rewarding and healthier to embrace your authentic self than to attempt to look and/or sound like someone you truly aren't.

The idea of finding your voice might seem strange at first, but it doesn't have anything to do with how you sound when you speak. In this context, your voice represents your core values, beliefs, and passions, as well as the way that you authentically express yourself to others and in your mind. Along with many other significant changes in the teen years, you can expect to become more independent and open-minded in your way of thinking and how you view the world. Your unique experiences and learning will shape and form your thoughts, ideas, and opinions so that they may be quite different from those of your immediate family members and close friends. These changes can potentially cause friction, especially when it comes to politics, social issues, and other potentially contentious topics. However, voicing your beliefs in an appropriate and respectful manner is an important part of your journey toward becoming self-assured and empowered to think independently.

Finding your voice also includes exploring, developing, and pursuing your passions. Though you definitely have responsibilities as a teen girl, you likely have a special kind of freedom as well when it comes to how you spend your time and effort outside of school, work, and chores. In other words, the teenage years often provide a wide window of opportunities for extracurricular activities such as sports, art, music, volunteering, and more. Participating in various activities can help you determine what you wholeheartedly enjoy and lead you to making connections and gathering ideas for pursuing your passions in the future.

Another positive element of the teen years is finding your personal style. This can encompass everything from the way you embrace fashion to your taste in movies and music to your approach to time management. Your personal style reflects how you present and express yourself to others as well as an avenue to let your inner spirit and personality shine. In addition, it's natural and advisable to try out different styles of self-expression when you are a teen girl to see what works for you and what doesn't. This might mean trying a new haircut, experimenting with different clothes or

13

makeup, or even considering a new genre of literature or gaming. As long as you are true to yourself, you will find a personal style that makes you happy.

It's also important to keep in mind that your voice and personal style are likely to change over time, so flexibility is key. For example, you may love certain colors and patterns at age 14 that won't necessarily fit your sense of style at age 18. This is to be expected, so be patient with yourself and continue to explore styles that make you feel fulfilled and comfortable. Flexibility is also essential when it comes to your voice in terms of following your passions and asserting your independent viewpoints. Keep in mind that your perspectives are likely to change as you gain wisdom and experience and be open to new ideas and diverse opinions.

Just like your identity, your voice and personal style will evolve along your journey of self-discovery. The teen years are a perfect time to find your passions and what is important to you, as well as how you wish to express yourself in an authentic way. Be brave, confident, flexible, and open-minded as you discover how unique and special you truly are.

# CHAPTER TWO: ALL ABOUT FRIENDSHIPS

Friendships are very important at all stages of life, but especially during the teenage years. Friends not only allow for social connections, fun, and experiences outside the immediate family, but they influence our overall health and well-being in many positive ways. However, friendships can also be incredibly complex and challenging during this teenage period, which is why it's helpful to understand good strategies to make meaningful friendships and maintain healthy relationships with friends.

There are many benefits to having meaningful, positive friendships. Friends offer us feelings of belonging and acceptance. For teen girls, good friends are a source of support that can offset negative experiences such as bullying and feelings of isolation or exclusion. This leads to greater happiness, self-confidence, and connection with others. Through friends, we learn about diverse approaches to family, culture, and other significant aspects of society. In addition, positive friendships can help us cope with difficult circumstances and reduce our overall stress. For example, if you experience a death within your extended family, such as a grandmother or grandfather, your friends are likely to offer support and love to help lessen your grief. They can also provide encouragement through challenging events such as an important exam or interview. Friends often inspire us to set and achieve meaningful goals as well, bringing out the best in our personalities and abilities.

Yet, for all the benefits that friendships can offer, it can be difficult to make friends and maintain these relationships. This is true at almost any age, including the teen years. For example, you may lose touch with the friends you had in elementary school once you get to middle or high school due to different classes or lunch schedules. In other instances, what you had in common with certain friends at one age may be less enjoyable at another age. Some people move to a different city or state, which can be stressful when it comes to starting and maintaining friendships.

Navigating any of these circumstances can feel overwhelming and discouraging at times. Therefore, it's important to have an understanding of how healthy and positive friendships are created and nurtured to make wonderful, lasting memories.

For most of your years as a teen girl, it's likely that school will be your main source of friendships since a large percentage of your time is spent in an academic setting. Some of your friends may carry over from elementary or middle school, but you may have opportunities as you get older to add people to your friend group or create different friendship circles altogether. As you know from learning about your journey of self-discovery, your identity will evolve significantly from ages 13 to 19. Your friends will experience this as well, meaning that your interests and priorities might take different paths. For example, you may be drawn more toward participating in your school's band or theater, whereas your good friend may decide to join an athletic team. This doesn't mean that your friendship should end, but it might change in unanticipated ways, which may require more effort on your part to stay connected. You may decide to eat lunch together on certain days or meet up on the weekend to remain close and maintain your friendship. In other instances, it's perfectly acceptable to allow a friendship to fade and keep the good memories with you.

In terms of making new friendships, it's wise to create a balance between outwardly seeking new friends and letting friendly relationships develop naturally. Some people are put off by those who seem too eager or desperate for instant friendship rather than allowing time to get to know one another and become compatible. For example, you may decide to join an after-school group or club at your community center that you find interesting. Ideally, the other participants would have similar interests, which can form the basis for good friendships. However, pressuring other members right away to exchange numbers or get together outside of scheduled meetings is probably too strong a strategy for making new friends. A better decision would be to smile and make interesting small talk at first to "break the ice." This can help you navigate being open and friendly while also allowing others to naturally reciprocate and get to know you.

It may seem difficult or intimidating to make new friends at an age when there is a heavy emphasis on social status, but please know that you are absolutely not alone. Though younger children tend to just outright declare friendship, most teens experience some form of social anxiety or awkwardness when trying to make friends. However, these feelings can dissipate as you grow more self-confident in your identity and develop interpersonal skills such as making conversation, offering support, and forming relationships outside your core family members. Some tools to consider are asking open-ended questions, actively listening to what the other person is saying, and being aware of social cues and body language. If someone doesn't seem willing or interested in becoming your friend, don't force the situation and try not to take it personally. That individual may be going through something that prevents them from seeing the value of your friendship, or they may just not be a good fit at that time.

Of course, it's not unusual for teens to make and maintain online friendships in addition to those in person. These relationships can have a very positive impact on both your digital and non-digital life to a certain extent. Because online friendships are limited in terms of communication and interaction, they should not completely replace or take precedence over in-person friendships. Therefore, it's ideal to keep a healthy balance between your online and offline friendships.

The bottom line is that making and maintaining friendships as a teen can be challenging and occasionally downright painful, but the benefits are definitely worth the patience, effort, and energy. Friends allow us to be our authentic selves in a way that is unique compared to other social groups, such as families, peers, and teammates. So, keep in mind that there are numerous people in the world who are willing to get to know and appreciate who you are, support and have fun with you, and create memories that last beyond your teen years.

# FINDING YOUR PEOPLE: QUALITY OVER QUANTITY

"Your people" refers to the friends that are closest to you and that are almost like family. Ideally, the members of your friendship group appreciate you for exactly who you are, support and uplift you when you need them and love to have fun and create memories with you. In return, you would treat them in the same meaningful way. It takes time to find and develop the friendships that become your tribe, and these relationships often change as you get older. Some friendships drift away while others grow even stronger, and your tribe may increase in numbers as you meet different people.

Like many things, some people may assume that having a lot of friendships is better than having just a few. Of course, it is nice to have a diverse and plentiful group of friends, but it's better to have a handful of positive and healthy friendships than lots of superficial relationships. One way to illustrate this and help you find your quality friend group is to consider the differences between friends and acquaintances.

An acquaintance is someone that you may see often but without sharing meaningful interactions or experiences. Relationships with acquaintances are usually casual, such as saying hello to the person who sits across from you in science class. Unlike a friend, it would seem strange to share something personal or emotional with an acquaintance — though a friendship can certainly develop between acquaintances over time. A friend is someone you trust and are connected to in an emotional way. Unlike an acquaintance, friends are people with whom you spend quality time and have meaningful conversations beyond small talk. Friendships require investments of time, energy, and commitment to build and maintain, which is why quality is much more important than quantity.

Since friendships provide so much in terms of support, empathy, and understanding, it makes sense that you would want to invest these qualities (and receive them in return) in a few close and reliable friends. There are many people with whom you probably enjoy spending time, talking, and participating in activities — and this is part of the fun of being social. However, when it comes to true friends with whom you can be open and vulnerable, it's far more beneficial to focus on the quality of their character rather than how many you have. This way, you'll be secure in knowing which of your friends are dependable and there to help you navigate through life and be part of wonderful memories.

A common notion is that finding a friendship group means forming a cohesive friendship circle in which everyone is close to each other. This can definitely be beneficial under the right circumstances, such as when everyone is on equal footing with trust and communication. However, it's also perfectly fine if the friends in your group are not close friends with each other. For example, you may have a best friend on your basketball team who doesn't really know the best friend you sit with at lunch each day. You can nurture each of these friendships in their own special way. It's also important to support your friends in maintaining their other friendships. This strengthens your quality as a friend and prevents any feelings of jealousy or resentment.

Keep in mind as well that there are as many types of friendships as there are friends, so you don't have to worry about sacrificing diversity when developing quality friendships. In other words, you are likely to make friends in many areas of your life beyond school, where you spend most of your weeks. This may include neighbors, co-workers, teammates, fellow online gamers, and other community members. These friendships are just as important as those you make in school because they are generally based on similar interests, and they deserve to be nurtured and maintained in the same way. No matter who is ultimately part of your circle, you should have quality friends that you can rely on, trust, and go to when you need support.

# BUILDING TRUST AND STRENGTHENING BONDS

Trustworthiness is one of the best traits to have as an individual and to find in a friend. Knowing that you can trust someone (and be trusted yourself) is not only comforting, but it allows for strong friendship bonds that are able to grow, last, and withstand little bumps in the road. However, trust and strong friendship bonds take time and effort to build and maintain, so it's helpful to approach true friendship with long-term thinking, patience, and perseverance.

One of the most important aspects of building trust is authenticity. Being authentic means that you are true to yourself and committed to your values and beliefs. Authentic people are also honest with others in what they say and do. For example, you may think that joining a certain club at school is a great way to make more friends. However, if you truly have no interest in the club's purpose or subject matter, you'll be an inauthentic participant, and eventually, that may reveal itself to the other members. This lack of authenticity on your part can lead to mistrust among others in addition to wasted time and effort for you. A better strategy would be to join a group, club, or team in which you have a genuine interest. You'll be more likely to meet friends who share the same interests and build a stronger foundation of trust through authenticity.

Another essential element when it comes to building trust is respect. In friendship, mutual respect allows each person to be themselves and still be accountable to each other. Respecting a friend includes being reliable, compassionate, loyal, and empathetic, all of which lead to a foundation of trust. For example, if a friend tells you something in confidence or private, it's respectful not to share the information with someone else unless you have permission to do so. In addition, if your friend invites you to go somewhere and you agree, it would be respectful to keep that commitment even if you are invited to something else. There are many other ways to show respect in friendship, such as being open in communication, actively listening, having a supportive and caring nature, taking responsibility for mistakes, and forgiving your friend for their mistakes.

Of course, it's important to remember that building trust involves effort from both parties of the friendship in addition to time, understanding, and dedication. Just as you are on a journey of self-discovery during your teen years, your peers and friends are undergoing something similar. If you notice that you are in a friendship that has drastically changed or become one-sided in terms of trust, then it's a good idea to evaluate the health of the relationship. For example, if you discover that one of your friends has become unreliable, inauthentic, or disrespectful toward you, it may be wise to limit the effort you put into the friendship until any misunderstandings are cleared up or until they fully reinvest in the friend partnership.

In addition to building trust, there are many positive ways to strengthen the bonds you have with your friends. One important and meaningful way to achieve this is through shared experiences. This can include activities that you and your friends enjoy doing together, opening up and expressing your thoughts and feelings, or even spending quality time as companions. Another way to strengthen your friendship bonds is to show that you genuinely care about your friend. Paying attention and genuinely getting to know them, offering unconditional support, and reaching out to them with a kind text or funny story will reassure your friend that they are important to you and in your thoughts.

Though most friendships go through some challenges and changes, overall, they should feel welcoming, natural, and reciprocal. If you end up realizing that you are consistently putting more effort into the relationship than your friend is, or if you feel that your friend views you as a last resort for hanging out, then you might be better off committing your energy to other friends who appreciate you more openly and sincerely. Trust and strong bonds with friends bring about mutual support, emotional comfort, and fun memories that can last a lifetime. These qualities must be established and embraced to make and maintain true and healthy friendships.

# THE ART OF COMMUNICATION

Like all relationships, communication, and understanding are the foundations of a positive friendship. Friends play significant roles in how we perceive our social acceptance and belonging, and friendships are a healthy way to develop empathy for and connection to others. The more we learn about our friends through open and shared communication, the greater our understanding of who they are as individuals and what their friendship means to us.

It may seem strange at first to think of communication and understanding as arts, but they both involve skill, practice, creativity, and personal expression. As your friendships grow and strengthen, so will your levels of meaningful interaction and appreciation for each other's uniqueness and subtleties. For example, you might share stories about how your family celebrates a certain holiday and find that your friend's experience with their family is entirely different. Balancing what you share, along with asking encouraging questions of your friends, is a cornerstone of communication as an art. In addition, actively listening to and remembering details shared by your friends will enhance your understanding of them as well as the strength of the friendship.

It can take a while at the beginning of a friendship to learn and understand each other's preferred types and methods of communication. For example, you may enjoy texting throughout the day, whereas your friend might be used to talking on the phone or over a video chat service. Or you may learn that your friend is sensitive to particular words or expressions and prefers that you avoid their use. This is where compromise comes in as you gain a deeper level of understanding of each other, as long as you both are willing to be flexible and adjust your approach to communicating. You may soon find that you and your friend have developed inside jokes with each other or even a "shorthand" way of speaking that is special between you.

Of course, miscommunications and misunderstandings are a natural part of any relationship, no matter how close you are or how long you've been friends. One way to navigate these issues before they become destructive or hurtful is to ask for clarification when you need it. For example, if your friend seems distant for a few days and it's causing you worry, it may be helpful to ask if there is something wrong or whether they need your support. This kind of open communication can help you and your friend clear up potential problems while also bringing you closer together through deeper understanding. It's also beneficial to be as patient, nonjudgmental, and encouraging as possible, as your friend may need time to open up. In return, your friends should feel comfortable getting clarification from you if they feel there has been a misunderstanding. The keys to maintaining long-term friendships are allowing for flexibility, mutual forgiveness, and even a sense of humor when it comes to misunderstandings or miscommunications.

Keep in mind as well that your body language conveys a form of communication, engagement, and understanding. If you appear disinterested, distracted or closed-off when your friend is trying to communicate with you, they may feel hurt or frustrated in response. For example, if you are scrolling on your phone while your friend is telling you about a significant event, you are likely to give the impression that you're ignoring them or that you don't care about their feelings. Therefore, it's important to give your full attention to your friends when having meaningful conversations so that they know you are encouraging, supportive, and focused on what they have to say.

The communication and understanding that evolves with friendship are special in many ways. It allows each person to share their thoughts and feelings in a welcoming manner, and it's also a way to celebrate each other's successes, strengths, values, and individuality. A trusted friend is someone you can confide in and know that they will respond with support and empathy, and it's equally rewarding to fulfill that role as a trusted friend for someone else. There is a common saying that friends are the family we choose for ourselves. That's why it's vital to nurture our friendships with communication, understanding, trust, and love.

# CHAPTER THREE:
# AVOIDING DRAMA

You may have heard the term "drama" as a descriptor for movies, plays, or some television series. In the teen years, the word drama can take on a completely different meaning. When we talk about navigating and avoiding drama, we mean those situations in which emotions are overly strong and interfere with rational thinking and behavior. In these situations, when ruled by emotion, people may say or do things that are hurtful toward others or that they later regret. Because the teenage years are marked by so many drastic changes, especially related to emotions, and many teens haven't fully developed the skills to cope with certain feelings and situations, it's no wonder that teens' lives may appear filled with drama.

We all occasionally find ourselves in dramatic situations when emotions run high. For example, you may have experienced drama with your family during the holiday season when people are feeling more emotional, tired, and sensitive than usual. Thankfully, these negative moments are usually brief and balanced with calm, fond memories as well as forgiveness. However, during your teen years, you may be spending more time with your peers and friends than with your family members. Since these people are independent of your family and probably haven't known you as long or as well, there is a greater chance of miscommunications and shifting dynamics in your relationships. And since your friends and peers are also going through similar emotional changes and developments, you may find yourself experiencing a different or more intense kind of drama in your interactions with them.

It can be difficult during the teen years not to get caught up in drama, whether it's in the form of gossip, romantic break-ups, friendship struggles, or something else. In fact, you may feel pressured to participate simply because it seems like everyone else is doing so or out of a natural instinct for curiosity or excitement. However, it's far healthier for your emotional and mental well-being to avoid drama if possible — and if you aren't able to avoid it, then it's good to know some strategies to help you navigate it without experiencing or causing any personal damage.

Though everyone goes through some dramatic moments, some people tend to attract or create drama more than others. These tendencies can be harmful to others in terms of self-esteem, social reputation, and long-term ability to trust. In addition, if you are associated or aligned with someone who enjoys drama, you may end up being part of the problem. For example, if you know a classmate who talks about their friends behind their backs or is regularly unkind to others, it's best to steer clear of them. If someone in your friend group starts outwardly excluding or making fun of others, these are other types of drama you should avoid as well. You may not feel confident enough to publicly call them out on their behavior, which could add to the drama, but you certainly have the option of excusing yourself and walking away or not participating by keeping silent.

As a teen girl, your social life is likely growing and expanding quickly. Though much of it will be rewarding and fun, you also might encounter people and/or situations that are difficult to navigate in a healthy way. For example, you may have a friend who pressures you, in public and private, to engage in risky behaviors such as alcohol or drug use. If you find yourself unable to handle certain circumstances in a productive or safe manner, make sure that you speak to a trusted adult. If they are not able to provide you with helpful guidance personally, then they are sure to direct you toward someone who can support you through any difficulties. Sometimes teens are uncomfortable discussing drama with adults because they worry about misunderstandings or misjudgments, but it's more likely that the adults you know and trust have been through similar situations. Therefore, they can offer their perspective and advice so that you have an easier time navigating any drama or avoiding it altogether.

# RECOGNIZING
# TOXIC RELATIONSHIPS

It can be difficult for anyone (including adults) to recognize when they are in a toxic relationship, whether it's with a friend, colleague, romantic partner, or even family member. However, these unhealthy relationships can take a serious toll on your emotional, psychological, and even physical well-being. Some toxic relationships can even lead to outright abuse and devastating harm that can take years to overcome. That's why it's essential as a teen girl to learn what constitutes toxicity so that you can avoid investing in relationships with such people or get yourself away from a relationship that is already in place.

Part of recognizing the signs of a toxic relationship is understanding the characteristics of a toxic person. In general, most people have a few toxic tendencies or traits from time to time because humans aren't perfect. However, if someone you know consistently displays demeaning or unhealthy characteristics without any acknowledgment, remorse, or effort to change, they are likely a toxic person and will carry that toxicity into their relationships. Some toxic traits are easy to spot as problematic and harmful, such as persistent dishonesty, anger, recklessness, aggression, and selfishness. Unfortunately, some people have toxic characteristics that are much more difficult to pinpoint as detrimental and unhealthy. These include excessive judgment, jealousy, negativity, arrogance, and/or passive-aggressive behavior.

Overall, toxic people tend to lack self-awareness as well as empathy for others. They show little concern for the feelings of other people. They may be manipulative, seeking to control others or ensure their own interests are served above anyone else. Some of these manipulative tactics may include ignoring or discounting what others say, attempting to discredit anyone who gets in their way, or even becoming aggressive when faced with opposition to their wants. Ultimately, if you feel a consistent lack of support, understanding, and compassion, or if you are threatened in any way (physically, emotionally, or psychologically), your relationship with that person is toxic and unhealthy.

Here are just some of the definitive signs that you are in a toxic relationship:

- You have been significantly harmed or injured in any way by that person.
- You feel threatened with harm or injury in any way by that person.
- You feel intimidated or fearful in the presence of that person.
- The person shows excessive jealousy or possessiveness.
- The person tries to isolate and prevent you from spending time with family and friends.
- The person attempts to control your social media, how you dress, what you say, or your participation in activities with others.
- Your self-worth or self-image has declined due to the other person's words and/or behaviors.
- The person has negatively influenced or interfered with your healthy relationships, academic progress, ability to perform tasks, or goal setting.
- You've lost interest in doing things or being around people that make you happy due to that person's words and/or behaviors.
- You feel consistently belittled or disrespected by the other person.

- You are unable to be your authentic self around the other person.

If you recognize that you are in a toxic relationship, get help and support immediately from your parents, guardians, school administrators, medical professionals, or even law enforcement if necessary. If you are not sure whether you are in a relationship with a toxic person, it's important to seek guidance from a trusted adult such as a parent, counselor, or teacher. They are likely to have some relevant life experience and can help you understand problematic relationships that may be harmful. In addition, they can offer guidance about effectively getting away from toxicity. Keep in mind that no relationship—friendship, romantic, or otherwise—is more important than your safety, health, and self-worth.

# SETTING BOUNDARIES

As you know, peer pressure can be difficult to navigate as a teen girl and result in a lot of drama. One way to counteract that is to learn to set boundaries and practice assertiveness. Boundaries, in this case, are personal "lines" that an individual metaphorically draws that indicate which behaviors they will tolerate and which they won't. For example, you may be uncomfortable giving people a hug when you first meet them, so you may set a personal boundary that you only shake hands as a greeting. Assertiveness is having the self-confidence and assurance to stand up for what you want or believe without being aggressive or offensive. For instance, if your co-worker is pressuring you to work an extra shift but you have important plans, an assertive response might be, "I am unable to work an extra shift due to a prior commitment, but I may be able to do so next time you ask."

Learning to set boundaries and practicing assertiveness takes time and experience, but these are very helpful strategies when it comes to navigating and avoiding drama. Both can be beneficial in dealing with peer pressure and not getting caught up in negative situations or high emotions. For example, before you go to a party with friends, it's wise to consider your personal boundaries in terms of participating in certain activities such as drinking alcohol or smoking. If you set a boundary that you won't do either, then you won't feel put on the spot or appear indecisive if they are offered to you. In general, people will respect your personal boundaries if you are clear and non-judgmental in stating them: "I appreciate the offer, but I don't drink anything that has alcohol in it." If someone does not respect your personal boundaries, then they may be a toxic person (see section above). In addition, it's important for you to respect your own personal boundaries with consistency so you don't lose credibility. In other words, if you assert that you don't smoke as a rule, then don't smoke.

Assertiveness comes from your inner confidence and self-awareness. As we grow and become more independent, we understand more about who we are, our likes and dislikes, and what we believe. This helps us make life choices and insulates us from outside pressures. The more you practice being assertive and trusting your choices, the more confident and decisive you will be, no matter what others are saying or doing. The key to being assertive is to avoid having a confrontational or aggressive tone. Simply state your preference clearly and with confidence.

As you become more self-aware and self-assured, you'll get used to establishing boundaries and responding assertively. This is part of developing your honest, authentic self. As a teen girl, you may feel pressured to take part in things that really don't interest you or make you feel comfortable. Of course, you can try new things if you are open to them — and saying that something doesn't interest you is not a clever way to get out of your responsibilities. Instead, setting boundaries and being assertive are tools that you can rely on to help you avoid peer pressure, uncomfortable situations, and unnecessary drama.

Sometimes, it won't be clear at first that a boundary needs to be set. Unlike situations like drinking, which are clearly against your values or outside of your comfort zone, there are circumstances that we don't immediately recognize as uncomfortable or in conflict with our true selves, even though they actually may be. One way to help you identify when to set boundaries with friends and family is to pay attention to when you feel resentment. For example, maybe your friend changes plans at the last minute. The first time this happened, you were disappointed, but it didn't seem like a big deal, so you said nothing. The second and third time it happened, though, you realized you were starting to feel resentment toward your friend. This is when it's time to set a boundary.

Boundaries are always focused on what you will do, not what another person will do. You can't make your friend less flaky or more organized, but you can be realistic about expectations. You might start this conversation by expressing how you feel. "I understand you are busy, but it seems planning ahead isn't working too well. I tend to give up on opportunities to keep that space available for you, and then I'm disappointed when you bail. From now on, I would prefer if you just text me on the day you want to hang out. If I'm available, I'll be more than happy to spend time with you!" This allows you to avoid this situation in the future while also allowing your friend the opportunity to still hang out.

This is a skill that will take practice. Sometimes, it will be hard to word what you want to say without sounding accusatory or defensive. If you are uncertain, try practicing what you want to say with a neutral friend or family member.

# HANDLING GOSSIP

Most people think of gossip as talking about someone who is not there in person for the conversation. Gossip can also include repeating information about someone or something that hasn't been verified as the truth. Though gossiping is typically considered a negative activity because it can be harmful and hurtful, humans have a natural instinct to participate in it. This is likely due to the importance of storytelling in the evolution of our cultural and social groups and the generally positive outcomes of sharing information.

However, when personal information is shared without permission or when such information is negative or untrue, gossip can be destructive. This is especially true today when rumors can get out of control and spread among a wide audience through social media. In terms of handling gossip when you hear it and someone else is the subject, the strategy is pretty straightforward: don't participate. This includes not reacting to it and definitely not repeating it. If someone asks whether you've heard a certain bit of gossip or whether you want to hear it, you can just reply that you aren't interested. You may feel a bit of peer pressure to participate, but if you resist, then you'll be at peace knowing that you didn't take any active part in spreading hurtful or untrue information.

Unfortunately, it can be more difficult to handle gossip if it concerns you, your friend group, or someone close to you. If you learn that you, personally, are the subject of some gossip, whether it seems hurtful or not, consider talking to a trusted adult about it.

This will not only give you a chance to express your feelings but also allow someone that you respect to support you and provide perspective. In most cases, it's best not to confront the person you believe may have started it or try to deny what was said to those who may have heard it. Though it might be tough in the short term, the best way to counteract gossip in the long term is to ignore it — like letting a fire burn out. This will help you retain your integrity and allow others to realize that you are above such silly, hurtful behavior.

In addition to harmful gossip, there are many experiences that teen girls go through that can result in very hurt feelings, such as feeling excluded, rejected, or misunderstood. Though it may seem backward, this is where the power of forgiveness can really help you feel better. Sometimes, we understand forgiveness as giving the person who has wronged us a "pass" or excuse for their behavior, so they won't continue to feel bad about what happened. We may accept someone's half-hearted apology or just ignore the hurt they caused as a means of getting over an awkward situation. However, that's just a small part of the act of forgiving. The true power of forgiveness is the strength and peace that it provides to you.

For example, let's say you find out that a friend who you previously trusted has spread a rumor about you that is untrue. This is an unfair situation, and you would be right in feeling hurt and betrayed in addition to angry at your friend. Whether they apologize or not, you may be reluctant to offer them forgiveness, understandably thinking that they'll "get away" with hurting you, forget what they've done, or even do it again. However, at this point, your forgiveness is for your benefit — not your friend's.

In other words, the power of forgiveness here enables you to let go of any anger or resentment over what happened so that it doesn't hurt you or preoccupy your thoughts any longer. There is a well-known comparison made about carrying a grudge or holding on to bitterness: it is like swallowing poison yourself in hopes that the other person becomes ill. By allowing yourself instead to forgive what happened and your friend's role, over which you had no control, you've embraced inner strength and a healthy response so that nothing related to the event has power or influence over you any longer.

# CHAPTER FOUR: EMOTIONAL WELL-BEING

There is a great deal of clarity for most of us in understanding what it means to achieve and maintain physical health. By the time you're a teenager, you are likely to know that eating a healthy diet, getting adequate rest, and exercising regularly will keep your body at a solid level of performance and wellness. In addition, you probably understand that going to a medical professional is a beneficial solution if you become sick or injured. What many people may not consider is that these principles should apply just as much to emotional health as they do to physical health.

Thankfully, attention to the importance of emotional health is gaining some traction, particularly when it comes to teenagers. Understanding emotional well-being and resilience is especially vital for teen girls, as internal changes can be just as drastic as any outward physical developments during this timeframe. In addition, teens may be far less prepared to cope with the complexities and challenges of emotional health than they are those of physical wellness. Therefore, it's essential to be aware of your emotional development and well-being, seek support from the right sources when you need it, and build resilience to effectively cope with and overcome life's challenges.

More than ever, young people face difficulties with emotional health that can lead to serious conditions such as anxiety, depression, addiction, and other disorders. Global concerns such as climate change, economic difficulties, and political injustice are prevalent each day for teenagers. Combined with personal struggles such as academic pressure, social acceptance, and unfamiliar hormonal changes, it's no wonder that teens report feeling overwhelmed and under-equipped to deal effectively with all that confronts them. Such an emotional toll can have negative effects on their self-perception and perspective of the world, which can impact overall health.

The good news is that researchers, educational professionals, medical personnel, parents, and others are more focused than ever on identifying and treating emotional health problems among the teenage population. Teens themselves also have a greater awareness of the importance of emotional well-being and where they might go for potential sources of support. This means that with the challenges associated with the teenage years, there is also potential for a greater understanding of how to instill and develop resilience and other coping mechanisms to avoid threats or damage to emotional well-being.

Your first line of defense when it comes to emotional wellness is you. Though most people are aware of the ups and downs that teenagers experience, nobody has the capacity to read your individual mind or know exactly how you are feeling in the moment unless you choose to express it. You likely have adults and friends who care a great deal about your overall health, but they may not be able to determine precisely when you are in need of emotional support or more direct care. Though it may feel awkward or uncomfortable at first, it's important to tell someone you trust if your emotions or thoughts seem out of control—especially if any potential harm to yourself or others is involved. The teen years are difficult enough to navigate without further isolating yourself or declining to seek help when you need it, and you will ensure a brighter and more successful path for your future by protecting and enhancing your emotional well-being in the present.

# DEALING WITH HORMONES

As you might know from biology class, hormones are chemicals that deliver "instructions" to the cells, tissues, and organs in your body. They are produced by glands within the endocrine system, and they regulate various processes in the body, such as growth, metabolism, immune function, and sexual reproduction, among others. Hormones are associated with the teen years because they direct the changes that happen during puberty in terms of physical growth and sexual development. The hormones that are responsible for puberty can begin having an effect as early as age 7 for girls, though the outward characteristics of puberty's onset are typically visible closer to age 13. Since each person grows and develops at a different rate and outcome during the teen years, it can be difficult to know when the hormonal changes due to puberty are completely finished.

Not only are hormones the catalysts for changing bodies and sexual feelings in teenagers, but they are also a powerful influence on emotions, impulses, and moods. Male and female teens are often described as "moody" or having mood swings, but in general, girls are more likely to express what they are feeling— either positive or negative—than boys. The experience of such intense emotional polarity across the teen years, understandably, can affect your self-esteem, decision-making, and relationships. These effects are often temporary, yet they can result in some lasting negative impressions and coping skills.

In addition, this roller coaster of emotions and hormones can impact behavior, especially in terms of diminished risk calculation. This is why teens sometimes participate in risky activities that can have negative effects, such as unprotected sex, drug or alcohol use, and other attention-seeking behaviors. Of course, this is an age range in which individuals are exploring their identities and futures, so some risk-taking is healthy in order to gain experiences and expand perspectives. However, there are some choices and decisions that teens might make on impulse that can adversely affect their future, including committing criminal acts or even posting something online that might draw negative attention from employers or college admissions.

Thankfully, there are strategies to help you deal with hormones, mood swings, and the overall emotional rollercoaster of teen girlhood — and to prevent you from making any drastic, impulsive errors. First, it's essential to establish a network of reliable people who can provide you with emotional support and honest communication. This can include your parents, siblings, other family members, teachers, counselors, coaches, friends, and anyone else who can offer you healthy guidance and wisdom when you feel emotionally adrift or uncertain in making a decision. In many cases, knowing someone is there to listen can comfort you and get you back on track. Second, it's helpful for you to develop some self-regulation strategies to manage your emotions and prepare for situations in which you may be confronted with impulsive decisions. For example, keeping a journal of your thoughts and feelings can give you a sense of calm, clarity, and control over your emotional health and reactions. In addition, before you go out with a group of friends or face certain types of peer pressure, it's helpful to set boundaries for yourself, as the previous chapter discussed.

Another important strategy is having patience and allowing yourself to get through any emotional upheaval as best as you can. This may involve embracing tears, laughter, and everything in between. You can expect to feel sad, angry, and frustrated as well as excited, happy, and energetic at different intervals throughout the days and weeks of being a teenager. The good news is that your hormones and mood swings will even out with time, so be sure to have self-compassion and practice self-care to promote your emotional well-being when you need it.

# BUILDING RESILIENCE

No matter how old, experienced, wealthy, or lucky you are, life will present challenges. Sometimes, these are small interferences like a storm temporarily knocking out the electricity or a store unexpectedly closing. At other times, challenges can feel overwhelming or insurmountable, such as facing a serious illness, loss of employment, or car accident. Unfortunately, there is no way to fully prepare for life's setbacks. However, building resilience as a teen girl is an effective way to cope so that future challenges don't derail your health, well-being, or path to success.

Resilience is an individual's ability to face and adapt to adverse conditions, stressful events, or even tragic situations. Some people use the image of a tree that bends in the presence of a strong wind to describe the concept of resilience. By bending rather than breaking, the tree is able to withstand the pressure of the wind until it subsides.

For a person, resilience usually refers to emotional and mental adaptability rather than physical pliancy. For example, you may have a setback in terms of a class at school and receive a less-than-desirable grade on an exam. Without resilience, you might decide that it's your teacher's fault for not presenting the material effectively or that you just can't understand the subject no matter what you do. However, with resilience, you can accept what has taken place and work to improve the situation in the future without dwelling on the aspects outside of your control. This may include finding a better way to study or joining a group for tutoring to better understand the subject and earn a more desirable grade the next time.

Some of the shared qualities of resilient people are the capacity for acceptance, understanding of purpose, and flexibility. Acceptance is a trait of resilient individuals in that they take responsibility for whatever part they may have played in a situation and take control of their response as well. Acceptance allows for the possibility of negative outcomes yet also supports each person's ability to make positive changes. Resilient people also have an understanding of purpose. This helps them focus on end goals without being derailed by challenges that may come up along the way. Being flexible is an important part of resilience in terms of adaptability in the presence of unexpected or unwelcome circumstances. This allows resilient individuals to change direction, regroup, and respond to difficulty with strength.

The teen years offer many hardships and challenges that can become opportunities to develop resilience. As a teen girl, you will navigate numerous relationships and activities as well as personal health, academic progress, and future paths. It's likely that you will feel emotionally overwhelmed at times by the unanticipated turns life can take. However, when you build resilience in response to adversity, you also develop coping skills and emotional strength so that you can overcome both present and future challenges.

For instance, let's say that you have worked hard to earn your driver's license by studying for the written test, taking driver's education classes, and practicing driving with a permit under the supervision of responsible adults. You have taken every opportunity to be successful in passing your driver's test and are looking forward to reaching an important milestone of independence and adulthood. Yet during the test, perhaps you feel nervous and forget to signal or brake properly, leading you to fail the exam. Of course, this would be extremely disappointing and emotionally distressing in the moment. You may feel resentful toward the test-giver or even want to blame the weather, other drivers, etc. However, a better way of coping would be to build resilience by accepting that you made some mistakes, regaining your purpose in earning your driver's license by trying again and showing flexibility in adapting to the slight delay in becoming an independent driver. This resilience will keep you on track and give you the emotional strength to persevere until you succeed.

# SEEKING SUPPORT

Just as you would seek professional medical advice and treatment for illness or injury or consult a coach or other expert for athletic training and skill-building, you should seek the same level of support and guidance when it comes to your emotional health. This can be done through therapy, counseling, and/or mentorship. Therapy is conducted by a mental health professional as a long-term method to treat mental health issues and/or alleviate emotional distress. Though counseling is related to therapy in some ways, it is more of a short-term experience conducted by someone who is a specialist who can help address a particular challenge or achieve a specific goal. Mentorship involves receiving guidance from someone who has experience in a certain area or field. Mentors often form a relationship with their mentees to share their knowledge, expertise, support, and connections.

When you are aware that you need emotional support, it's advisable to first speak with a trusted adult to determine what type of help would benefit you most. For example, if you feel that your emotional health is preventing you from filling out college applications or meeting admissions deadlines, a reputable school counselor may be the best fit to help you overcome those feelings and get on track. If you are overwhelmed at starting a new job or deciding on a long-term career, finding a mentor would likely give you some insight as to how to proceed and support you in the process. If your emotional health is drastically suffering or you feel at a loss in terms of your well-being, exploring therapy might be a good choice to assist you in identifying and healing the causes of your distress.

Some teens may have difficulty in expressing or pinpointing a decline or problem with emotional health. Unlike a physical issue, it can be difficult to indicate what "hurts" or feels wrong. You may decide to stick things out until you feel better or hope that your situation will improve with time. These strategies can work in some instances. However, if you know that your emotional well-being is not improving or if it's getting worse, then it's time to seek support from professionals or other qualified individuals. Addressing your concerns and feelings as soon as possible will not only help you get on track to better emotional health, but it will prevent any problems from becoming worse in the meantime.

Don't worry if you aren't initially sure where exactly to seek support or what type of professional would work best for your situation. The first step would be to let a trusted adult know that you feel the need to address your emotional health. Some options for such an adult would include a parent or other family member, school counselor or psychologist, teacher, coach, or other reliable adult. They may ask you some questions about your feelings and experience in order to help you find the right source of support, so try to be as honest as you can. Remember as well that there are numerous people and services out there designed to assist with emotional health issues, so if you aren't matched with the "right" one at first, there will be other options.

Seeking support for emotional health has historically come with social stigma, meaning a perception of disapproval by society. Some people you know may continue to be under the impression that professional help for emotional well-being is unnecessary or unimportant. However, that's a very short-sighted viewpoint. The need for emotional health and related services is equal to, if not greater than, that for physical health, and this is especially true during the teen years when emotional turmoil is so often present. So, no matter what anyone says, trust your instincts when it comes to getting the support that you need.

# SELF-CARE

At the risk of redundancy, it's important to keep in mind that there is a clear link between self-care and emotional well-being. Burnout, depression, and anxiety can occur when our minds and bodies are under too much stress for too long of a time. Taking care of your physical body can help with this.

Exercise is known for releasing endorphins, which are essentially hormones that help you feel happy. It's recommended to get at least 45 minutes of exercise three times a week. This doesn't need to happen all at once. If you don't have 45-minute chunks of time, you can opt for three 15-minute stints. One way to fit this into a busy schedule is to take 15-minute breaks every two hours to dance, strength train, or walk around outside.

Sleeping eight to ten hours a night will dramatically improve how your brain functions during the day. If you don't get enough sleep, you are more likely to experience brain fog and find your temper a little shorter than usual. If you make a habit of not getting enough sleep, your immune system will weaken, increasing your chances of getting sick. In addition to this, if your mind and body are not performing as well as they should, you are more likely to experience compounding issues. For example, being late for school one time is most likely not a big issue, but forming a habit of it can impact your grades and, in turn, your self-esteem and feelings of worth.

Burnout happens when we pack too much into our schedule for too long. We currently live in a hustle culture that encourages people to constantly accomplish goals. It can be easy to get to a point where you don't have any real free time. Even if some of this time is spent socializing with friends, it can slowly wear you down to constantly be "on the go."

Unfortunately, if burnout isn't addressed immediately, it can become chronic. When this happens, it takes longer to resolve burnout, and it comes back frequently with more intensity. When burnout occurs, it's a good idea to ground yourself. Take your responsibilities down to the bare minimum when you start to feel overwhelmed. If you have extracurriculars, figure out which ones you can skip without long-term effects. For example, if you are on a team, talk to your coach and ask them if it's okay to skip a practice or two. If you have community engagements, call and see if you can find someone to take over some of your tasks for you until you feel better. Instead of going out, ask your closest friend to come over and do something relaxing, like watching a movie.

Hygiene can also be a great way to lower your stress and care for your mental health. When you are feeling overwhelmed, sad, or stressed, try taking a hot bath or shower. Spend some extra time grooming yourself and see about getting some special care items like face masks, hair masks, a bath bomb, or a new nail polish. These shouldn't be expensive, just a little touch of luxury to add to your day.

The key to this section is to slow down and focus on the basic building blocks of your life until you feel better. Preventive care is better than getting to a point where your body and mind shuts down. It's much better to ask for a couple of practices off or to temporarily pass duties off to another person and have it planned out than to get to a point where you can't follow through with your commitments. Most people understand if you need a temporary break and ask for it ahead of time. They're usually less responsive, though, if you just don't show up or fail to follow through unexpectedly. A good example of this is at work. If you know you are overwhelmed, finding someone to cover your shifts is much better than running into a situation where you have to call out the day of your shift. The more you learn to recognize when you need a break and take steps to create the space for one responsibly, the better you and everyone around you will feel.

# CHAPTER FIVE: DATING AND RELATIONSHIPS

As you grow into the teenage years, you are likely to find yourself (to some degree) in the world of dating and relationships. This presents exciting opportunities to get to know other people as well as yourself on a level different from friendship. Dating and romantic relationships can make you feel appreciated and special, yet they can also be emotionally challenging and confusing. That's why it's important to understand what you may be feeling, the necessity of personal boundaries, and how to deal with heartbreak so that you can move forward—just in case.

The concept of today's dating world, compared to that of your parents, older siblings, or even Hollywood portrayals, has changed. In a traditional sense, dating is when you spend time with someone, doing activities to have fun together and get to know each other, as a means of "testing out" whether there might be romantic feelings or the possibility of a stronger relationship. However, a majority of teenagers today consider a "dating" status to imply that a relationship has already begun. Most would describe the period before dating as "talking" or "hanging out." Another big difference is the way current teenagers meet and interact with each other, which is often through social media and text messaging. This can present challenges when it comes to face-to-face contact and in-person communication.

What hasn't changed, however, is the fact that developing "crushes" or even being part of official romantic relationships brings with it a whirlwind of emotions and experiences. On top of navigating physical and psychological changes during these years, the dating world can be overwhelming for teenagers with its incredible highs and upsetting lows. As a teen girl, it's more important than ever that you seek advice, guidance, and support when you need it to help you navigate these new feelings, relationships, and situations.

You may find that some adults tend to downplay or minimize the significance of romantic feelings and relationships during the teen years. They might refer to it as "puppy love," infatuation, or just a crush. This is primarily because most "first loves" don't tend to last into adulthood. However, the experiences you have with dating as a teen are actually very important and can help you avoid problematic relationships in the future. They can also provide meaningful insight in terms of who you are as a person, what characteristics you value in a romantic partner and/or relationship, and how to approach love and all that comes with it beyond the teen years.

# INFATUATION VERSUS LOVE

Part of the learning curve in the teen years, and often beyond, is being able to differentiate between infatuation and love. Infatuation is typically a short-term period of intense emotional passion and/or admiration for someone that can feel all-consuming. For example, you might recognize feelings of infatuation that you may have had for a celebrity at one point. Infatuation is often felt at the beginning of a dating or romantic relationship, and people usually describe this phase with terms like being smitten or head over heels. Love is more of a long-term, steady, and quiet emotion that you feel for someone who you've grown to know well over time. This doesn't mean that love can't be thrilling or passionate because it often is. However, compared to infatuation, love tends to reflect an attachment that is deeper and more enduring.

Although understanding the difference between infatuation and love is valuable, it's more important to focus more on recognizing the way they may affect your thought processes and judgment. Infatuation tends to be based more on fantasy, such that the other person's complexities and flaws are often idealized or overlooked. For the most part, love is based on reality, with the recognition that the other person is a human that possesses both negative and positive qualities.

A loving relationship allows both parties to be their authentic selves through acceptance and dedication. When you have an understanding of these differences, you can examine whether your feelings for someone are based on who they truly are as a complex individual or an idealized version of who you think they are. This can help you maintain logic and reason so that you are less susceptible to poor decision-making or impaired perception in navigating the dating world.

One helpful way to distinguish between these two concepts is to consider that infatuation is a state of mind and love is a state of being. Much of what happens when you are infatuated is one-sided and actually takes place in your internal thoughts and emotions. This doesn't mean that what you are thinking or feeling isn't real. However, it does mean that your perspective and interpretations may heavily influence the way you perceive experiences and events while infatuated. In other words, infatuation is often short-lived and is a period in which you might ignore someone's negative qualities or dismiss their true nature, even if the signs are very clear. Love, unlike infatuation, allows you to view someone in their entirety. You can appreciate their good qualities while also understanding and accepting their flaws, just as they would for you.

The fairy tale Cinderella is a great example of infatuation that can cloud someone's judgment and interfere with their logic. As the story often goes, the prince is enamored with Cinderella at the ball because of her beauty and grace. In nearly every version, he doesn't even know her name or where she lives but is certain that she is the one he wants to marry. On the other hand, Cinderella flees from the ball at midnight before she turns from a princess back into a scullery maid. This is because she recognizes at some level that the prince is infatuated and perceives her magical image as "perfect." If Cinderella believed that the prince genuinely loved and accepted her for who she truly was at the ball, she would have felt no need to run away once her appearance changed from riches to rags. Of course, fans of this tale are led to believe that Cinderella and the prince lived happily ever after in love once they found each other again and got married. Yet this isn't specifically portrayed in the story because developing a relationship based on love often takes a long time and a lot of hard, unglamorous effort.

Whether you are feeling infatuation, love, or both, dating relationships can be a wonderful part of the teen years. Connecting with someone on a romantic level for the first time is a memorable experience that brings with it a lot of excitement, joy, and intense emotion. However, it's also important to protect yourself as much as possible from losing your balance and putting all your attention, energy, and effort into a dating relationship. The truth is that most teen romances don't last into adulthood, whereas your relationships with friends and family members probably will. Therefore, it's essential to keep investing care and attention in yourself and those close to you, as well as the person who has currently won your heart.

One way to navigate this stage between infatuation and love is to give your new relationship a three-month period before making a final decision on whether a person is a good match for you or not. If both of your feelings remain constant through the first three months, there is a good chance it's not just the initial rush of hormones and excitement. It can be hard to keep your focus during the first weeks of a new relationship. A good practice to develop is to dive deep into your hobbies, friends, and family during the early stages. This will create space for your mind to process the relationship objectively and also set up the relationship for a healthy start. It will make it easier for both of you to maintain your identities and commitments as well as balance the relationship in terms of personal needs. Neither of you should "need" each other in any significant way within the first months. Interdependence comes later when the bond has matured past the initial stage.

# BOUNDARIES
# WHEN DATING

Setting boundaries is essential when it comes to dating relationships. Boundaries are limits and/or rules that you put in place for yourself and other people within a relationship. For example, you might set a boundary that you will be home by 11:30 p.m. on non-school nights or that your date must meet your parent(s) before you go out for the first time. This is for your emotional health, mental well-being, and physical safety. When you are starting out in the dating world, your parents or other caregivers may put strict rules in place as far as when you can go out, where you can go, and who you can date. This may seem unfair at first, or you may feel as if you aren't trustworthy in their eyes, but most of the time, it is for the benefit of your protection. As you get older and gain more dating experience, you are likely to take over setting boundaries in your relationships to prioritize your well-being and preserve your sense of self.

Though you won't be able to anticipate every situation when you start dating, there are some circumstances that you might expect to arise. Setting boundaries for yourself ahead of time will keep you from having to make decisions on the spot or during the infatuation phase when you may not be thinking as clearly.

Therefore, it's healthy to keep a list or make journal entries about what you want from a dating relationship and what would be unacceptable. For example, you might consider that it's best to maintain your friendships while dating so that you have balance and support in terms of your social life. Asserting that your friends will remain a priority before you start dating someone will help you set and keep that boundary in place. Other boundaries to consider may include setting times to focus on academics, sports, work, and family life—especially since new dating relationships can be so immersive and distracting. Ultimately, the goal of setting boundaries in relationships of any kind is not to take away any of the fun or limit new experiences but rather to ensure your health, safety, and self-respect are preserved.

It's also wise to consult trusted adults for advice on more significant boundaries before you begin a dating relationship. This may seem awkward or difficult at first, but their experience and wisdom can help you navigate ways to keep yourself safe and healthy. For example, your parents may expect you to abide by a curfew or check in periodically with your phone to ensure that certain boundaries are in place while you are on a date. A trusted adult may also recommend that you set clear boundaries in terms of alcohol, smoking, and other substances so that you aren't pressured into participating in unhealthy behaviors. Of course, one of the biggest challenges in dating relationships is setting and adhering to physical boundaries. If you aren't sure what is expected, appropriate, or comfortable for you in terms of sex or physical intimacy, reach out to an adult who has your best interests in mind. They can help you figure out healthy limits and how you can maintain them if you happen to be confronted with pressure to go beyond those limits. It's a good idea that this person is older than you. Your peers don't have enough experience yet to knowledgeably speak on the emotional and physical risks of going too fast too soon. Look for someone to confide in who is older than

26 (as their brains have fully developed and they've gained life experience) and who you genuinely respect. Never forget that it is your right and prerogative to set clear boundaries at any time, assert those boundaries, and protect yourself from anyone who does not respect them.

No relationship is more valuable than your health, safety, and self-worth. Not only is it potentially dangerous in the moment to compromise your values and boundaries for someone else, but such decisions can result in harmful patterns and negative effects for your future. Though it may sound cliché, anyone who doesn't respect your personal boundaries does not have respect for you as a person. Of course, this refers to people that you date, but it also includes you. Respecting and committing to your own personal boundaries are part of respecting yourself, and that self-respect will enhance your confidence, decision-making, and long-term resilience during and beyond your teenage years.

# DEALING WITH HEARTBREAK

Unfortunately, heartbreak is pretty much an inescapable human experience—especially when you are new to the world of dating and romance. Allowing yourself to be vulnerable in a relationship with someone else in terms of your thoughts and feelings can be very exciting and rewarding. However, if someone doesn't appreciate your vulnerability, rejects your affection, or treats you carelessly, that can cause a great deal of heartache and self-doubt. In addition, the fact that almost everyone goes through heartbreak at some point may provide a little comfort.

Though heartbreak can be painful and stressful, it's important to remember that it won't last forever. Depending on the circumstances, some break-ups may be more difficult to put behind you than others. Some break-ups require more time to heal from. However, there are strategies that you can utilize to help you get through a broken heart and move forward. Most importantly, you need to prioritize your self-care as you deal with heartbreak. This means putting your health and well-being first, physically, emotionally, and mentally. Therefore, it's essential that you get regular, quality sleep in addition to eating as healthy as possible and getting some exercise each day to take care of your mind and body. Doing activities or participating in hobbies that you enjoy can also provide emotional stability. Continue to focus on your academic courses, extracurriculars, and/or job to feel productive, and attempt to alleviate stress in healthy ways such as taking walks, reading, or practicing yoga. The more care and love you give yourself during this period of heartbreak, the more resilient you will feel.

It's also essential to spend time with people who love and appreciate you, such as your family and friends. This will bolster your self-esteem, keep you focused on the present, and allow you to receive genuine support when you need it. Talking about your feelings is important but be sure to also focus on topics that are unrelated to your heartbreak to help normalize your thoughts and behavior patterns again. Allow yourself time to cry, grieve, and express anger, and if you feel the need for professional help, then don't hesitate to ask for it. Be sure to allow yourself time to do things that you enjoy, whether it's a productive activity or just a distraction so that you aren't stuck in negative emotions for a prolonged period.

Unfortunately, social media can greatly interfere with getting over heartbreak and moving forward. It can be tempting to frequently check on your "ex" and examine their profiles and pictures to see if they are miserable or have moved on from the relationship. Though this may feel helpful in the moment as a means of reassurance or staying connected, tracking your ex through social media is generally harmful and a hindrance to your emotional healing. There is a common phrase that might give you insight in terms of moving forward without monitoring your ex online: *To heal a wound, you have to stop touching it.* It's far more beneficial for you to wish them well, let them go, regain your sense of self, and find your path forward. If you find yourself tempted to scour social media pages or if you get stuck looking at profiles, do something else immediately. This can include calling a friend, writing in your journal, or watching a new movie or series so that you don't delay or disrupt the healing process by looking backward.

Finally, though it may seem like a good solution to start dating again right away or jump into another romantic relationship, it's wise to go slowly and embrace the healing process first. For as awful as heartbreak can be as an experience, it's also a chance for you to gain insight about yourself and grow as a person. A large part of moving forward is taking time to reflect on what you've learned and how you can better navigate future relationships. Take opportunities to reconnect with family, friends and activities that make you feel valued and appreciated. Above all, remember that the longest, closest, and most meaningful relationship you'll have in your life is with yourself, so be sure to treat yourself with kindness, patience, and care.

# CHAPTER SIX:
# PLANNING FOR
# THE FUTURE

The teen years can be an exciting time for several reasons, one of which is considering the many opportunities that will be available to you in the future. Though it's impossible to know for sure the person you'll be in adulthood or the life circumstances you'll face beyond the teenage years, it's beneficial to make general plans for your future so that you have some agency, direction, and insight when it comes to making important choices. By the time you reach age 20 and are no longer a teenager, you are likely to already be on the path of higher education, career building, and/or forming lifelong relationships. The more time you put into thinking about and planning for your adult journey, the greater your success will be.

Of course, it can be intimidating to map out your future at such a young age, especially when you aren't sure what kind of life choices are ahead of you or what you ultimately will want to do. Thankfully, you aren't expected to have a comprehensive plan ready to be followed exactly on your last day of being 19 years old. Instead, planning for the future in the teen years means learning what interests you and what doesn't, the things that inspire you, and potential paths to take that can help you reach your dreams and goals as they develop and change.

Thinking about how to plan for your future is also an opportunity for you to connect with the important adults in your life by asking them questions and listening to stories about their journey from teenager to adulthood. Consider talking to your grandparents, parents, aunts, uncles, neighbors, and even your teachers and coaches to find out what situations they faced and what decisions led them to where they are. Even if you don't end up following similar paths, you will benefit from hearing about your loved ones' knowledge, wisdom, and experience. You'll also develop a greater understanding of who they are, which can lead to more meaningful connections and relationships.

Remember that you have the flexibility of time as well as the freedom and capacity to change your mind about everything from what you want to do to where you want to go. So, rather than feeling pressured to map out a rigid outline for your future, it's wise to embrace opportunities and experiences as they come to develop insight and understand your authentic self. In this way, you can patiently and naturally approach planning your future as you develop a wonderful, forever friendship with yourself.

# SETTING GOALS

Developing the habit of setting short-term and long-term goals is one of the most potentially rewarding strategies you can learn in your teenage years. Overall, goals are a way of establishing and defining outcomes and results that you intend to accomplish. They also help keep you focused, motivated, and accountable in your progress toward achievement. Some people prefer to set large, general goals such as entering a certain career field or traveling to another part of the world. Others tend to set smaller and more specific goals, like getting a closet organized or increasing practice hours each week for playing a musical instrument. Whether large or small, short- or long-term, setting goals for yourself is an important life skill that will give you purpose, direction, and an enhanced likelihood of success for whatever you choose to do.

You probably already have experience in setting and achieving informal goals. For example, you may have saved enough of your allowance over a few weeks to buy a new video game, or you may have worked your way up to running a certain distance in a physical education class. However, by learning how to set concrete goals and designing specific steps and plans to achieve them, you'll gain even more advantages in terms of what you can accomplish. A concrete goal is one that you clearly define so that you know exactly the result you intend to reach. This is helpful because it specifically identifies the outcome you want and then allows you to prioritize and concentrate on the actions needed to make it happen. For example, you might want to set an overall goal of reading more books during the summer. This is an excellent intention, but it lacks a specific and concrete outcome, which can make the goal difficult to measure and achieve. Clearly defining your reading goal, such as dedicating 20 minutes per day to reading or checking out and finishing a new library book each week, makes it much easier in terms of planning, focusing, and achieving results.

The difference between short-term and long-term goals may seem straightforward or obvious, but it's important to distinguish between them so you can take the best approach. In general, short-term goals are specific, relevant, and can be achieved in the near future. For example, if you want to improve your math grade before the end of the semester, you might set that as a short-term goal and then create a workable plan to reach it within that semester's timeline. Steps that you might outline to help you achieve an improved math grade may include working with a tutor, increasing your study time, enhancing your study habits, consulting with your teacher, and paying closer attention during class time. If your math grade improves, then you'll know that the short-term goal you set and the plan you made to achieve it was effective. If your math grade doesn't improve, then it would be important to reassess your goal setting and achievement strategies to find a more successful approach and method.

Unlike short-term goals, long-term goals tend to be more generally defined, adaptable and pursued over a lengthier period of time. It can be more challenging as a teenager to set long-term goals since you may be unsure of exactly what you want to accomplish in the future. Therefore, it's wise to keep this type of goal more general in its definition, with room for you to adapt the steps and plans for reaching it. One example of a long-term goal that many teens set for themselves is attending college or a university after graduating from high school. If this is one of your goals, and your high school graduation is a few years away, then you would outline general steps to reach it in the long term. For example, you might plan at first to earn good grades, participate in sports and activities, and volunteer for community service to start building leadership and experience. As you get closer to the college application process, you might include steps such as researching colleges that interest you, consulting with your academic counselor, taking note of application deadlines, and asking for letters of recommendation. Of course, you can remain flexible with this long-term goal as you may decide to delay going to college in favor of something else. However, organization, planning, and productivity will benefit you no matter what you decide.

# EXPLORING CAREER PATHS

As a teenager, the future can seem a bit intimidating. For some, the thought of being an independent adult is exciting, whereas for others, it can feel downright scary. You can be reassured that you aren't expected to know the career path you intend to follow or the degree you'll end up pursuing until you actually get there, so you can alleviate that pressure in your mind. Instead, you have the luxury of time and energy as a teen girl to explore all the potential career and educational paths that will make your journey as an adult fulfilling, interesting, and rewarding.

There are many productive ways to explore future career and training possibilities, as well as subjects to study and degrees to earn. You probably encounter different positions and ideas in your daily life just by observing occupations and getting to know a variety of people. Consulting your high school guidance or career counselor is another way to gain insight as to what paths are available to you in the future. In addition, there are a few reliable "aptitude" tests online that can reveal education, career, and even vocational trajectories for which you may be suited. Some colleges and universities allow individuals to audit certain classes, which is another way to explore what might interest and inspire you. It's important to keep an open and flexible mind as well as recognize your talents and passions so that you don't limit your possible choices.

Though it may seem counterintuitive, learning what you are not interested in as far as career paths and educational opportunities is as valuable as exploring what appeals to you. This can help you narrow down your options in a big way. For example, if you consistently dread or are bored with a certain subject in school, then there's a good chance that you wouldn't want to pursue that area of study when you get to college (though your interests may change). In addition, if you have no interest in a certain career field, a particular type of job, or one that requires a specific skill set, then you are likely to avoid pursuing that in the future. For example, you may feel reluctant when it comes to a lot of public speaking and decide to look for careers in which that activity is minimal. Though it's always a good idea to maintain an open mind, it's perfectly fine to acknowledge and accept what doesn't interest or work for you. That way, you can spend your time and energy on what truly suits who you are.

Remember that you can always change your mind as your interests develop and as you discover more about yourself. It's unrealistic for anyone, including yourself, to expect to know exactly what you

wish to study after high school or pursue as a career in the future —
especially during the teen years. However, there are a lot of
benefits to exploring your potential and the many opportunities
that are and will be available to you in terms of higher education,
vocational training, and a rewarding career as an adult.

# MENTORSHIP AND
# ROLE MODELS

Having role models and interacting with mentors is not only
beneficial for your future education and career goals, but these
relationships can also reduce stress, inspire confidence, and
improve your overall health and well-being. Role models and
mentors are valuable in helping to shape your future goals and
plans as well as define clear courses of action to achieve your
dreams. There are successful individuals in all areas of life who
would at least partially attribute their accomplishments to a role
model and/or mentor.

A role model is someone that you would consider to be a good
example of what you personally would like to achieve or aspire to
be in terms of character traits, life skills, or position in society. For
example, if you dream of becoming a writer, your favorite authors
would likely be role models. Most people have several role models
that inspire them to consider big possibilities. Role models can be
people you know and look up to in real life, such as teachers and
coaches, or they can be public figures that you admire for the
examples they set, such as activists and artists.

A mentor is someone with whom you have a personal relationship
based on their expertise, experience, leadership, and guidance.
Where role models are informal, mentors usually have a more
formal edge to them. Regardless of the direction you are headed,

finding someone to mentor you is important for getting advice and navigating higher education. If there is a teacher or authority figure you admire, create a list of specific questions to ask them. This will help start a relationship. Remember, their time is valuable, so think about what you want to know about regarding their success before approaching them. Depending on the context of the relationship, you may only talk to a mentor a handful of times or meet consistently for guidance.

A good example of how role models and mentors differ is to think about artists. If you were a writer and you wanted a role model, you could choose anyone with more experience than you that you know, even a classmate who is succeeding with their writing practice. You might share ideas and emulate their process. A mentor might include an author you particularly enjoy. To pursue a mentor relationship with them, you might write them a letter or attend a book signing where you can ask specific questions about their craft, process, and career path. If you were a musician, a role model might be anyone with more experience than you in your immediate community (think a local band member, an older kid at school who can show you something new, or a relative who plays the same instrument) whereas a mentor might be a professor or a professional musician you reach out to for more formal instruction. Engagement with a celebrity role model might mean reading or listening to all of their work, paying attention to interviews where they give advice, and emulating their style in your own practice.

Today's access to technology, information, and numerous avenues of communication can ease the burden of finding mentors and role models. There are a variety of companies, businesses, and other organizations that offer mentorship programs for those who are interested and willing to reach out. These programs often provide learning opportunities, networks for leadership and guidance, and even potential internships for more direct or hands-on experience.

Many colleges and universities offer mentorship programs as well to enhance student success and long-term achievement.

# CHAPTER SEVEN:
# EMPOWERMENT AND
# LEADERSHIP

One of the greatest rewards as you transition through the teen years to womanhood is gaining empowerment and developing leadership. These traits will build your self-confidence, open up exciting opportunities, and set you on a rewarding and successful path for your future. For example, your effort and dedication to a certain sport may result in becoming a captain or other type of team leader. Or you may be involved in scouting and have the chance to inspire and lead younger members. It does take courage and effort to become empowered and take on leadership roles as a teen girl, but the benefits are truly worth it.

Empowerment and leadership are similar concepts, yet they have their differences. Empowerment means that you inherently understand the ability to exercise your freedom and authority as an individual. This is an especially important tool for women, as their gender has not always been empowered on an equal level. Today's young women, in most cases, are empowered to make decisions regarding their future and control their autonomy. However, society is not perfectly equitable yet, which is why female empowerment should be embraced, appreciated, and strengthened when possible. Leadership is more of an external quality that allows individuals to motivate and positively influence others to reach a common goal. Thankfully, more women are taking on more leadership roles than ever in several areas of society, such as politics, science, business, education, and art.

Some teenagers take on empowerment and leadership roles very naturally, whereas others may need more time to learn these valuable traits through observation and experience. No matter where you fall on this scale, the root of empowerment and leadership is confidence in yourself. This might seem difficult to achieve in the teen years as you face new changes and challenges each day on top of trying to figure out your sense of self and place in the world. However, as you grow physically, emotionally, and intellectually, you will become more self-assured, capable of making decisions, and clear in your perception of who you are. These are all characteristics of women who are leaders and empowered individuals.

Ultimately, empowerment and leadership are not about controlling others, taking up the spotlight, or pushing to get your own way. Instead, these qualities are meant to inspire you to reach for your dreams and goals without setting limitations on yourself simply because you are part of a certain gender, race, culture, etc. Utilizing your empowerment and leadership skills can have a positive impact on your community and beyond. In addition, putting these qualities to good use will inspire others to feel empowered and accomplish their own goals.

# TAKING CHARGE:
# LEADERSHIP QUALITIES

There are many positive ways to cultivate leadership qualities in your teen years. This doesn't mean that you have to be elected president of your class or run for local office. Leadership skills can be utilized in almost any situation, large and small. This includes applying the qualities of a leader to yourself as a means of motivation, setting goals, and staying on task. Perhaps the most important leadership quality that you can cultivate is being your authentic self. When others recognize that you are genuine, truthful, consistent, and able to stand by your beliefs, they will trust your words and actions. This will also demonstrate that you are reliable, dependable, and credible—all traits that excellent leaders possess. Sometimes, it can be difficult as a teen to remain authentic and true to who you are, especially when facing peer pressure to conform to certain trends or join in what seems like popular behaviors. However, the more dedicated you are to your authentic self, the easier it will be to remain true to your beliefs and values as a true leader.

Leaders are also active listeners and empathetic to others. This means that they focus on what others are saying and respond in a non-judgmental way that shows understanding. Working on your interpersonal and communication skills is an excellent way to develop your listening abilities and empathy toward others. For example, you might notice a new student in some of your classes. Getting to know them by striking up conversations and paying attention to their thoughts and feelings will not only potentially lead to making a new friend but also help you refine the way you interact with and learn from others. In fact, being approachable is one of the strongest traits among effective leaders. Leadership is also based on demonstrating respect for people, keeping an open mind to new ideas and information, and showing a willingness to collaborate.

Of course, gaining experience in leadership roles is also a means of cultivating these qualities. It can be hard to know where to begin or how to find a leadership position, but being aware of and open to opportunities is a good initial strategy. You may decide to start small by leading a group project at work or in school and learn from that experience. Another possibility to help you get started is to look for opportunities to be a co-leader with someone else so that the responsibilities are shared. Almost any group, team, or community activity requires various levels of leadership, and the more responsibility you take on, the more experience and knowledge you'll gain for future roles as a leader.

Even if you aren't sure what type of leader you would like to be or how to implement your leadership qualities, it's important to be active and engaged with your community and support the causes you believe in. You can also find role models who set good leadership examples to inspire and guide you toward your own goals of being a leader. If you have a mentor or an adult in your life whom you admire, they may also be a source of teaching leadership techniques and presenting opportunities for you to take on such a role. Ultimately, you have the chance to make a positive difference and encourage others to accomplish their goals by embracing your own self-confidence and working toward becoming a leader that is respectful, authentic, and competent.

# CLUBS, ORGANIZATIONS, AND MOVEMENTS FOR CHANGE

One of the most exciting aspects of being a teen girl right now is the wealth of opportunities available to develop leadership skills and participate in meaningful groups with positive goals. There are a variety of clubs and organizations that support movements for change to make society more equitable and bring awareness to the need for advancements and improvements for the overall benefit of people, animals, and the planet. Joining any of these clubs, organizations, or movements is an excellent and rewarding opportunity to make a difference in your future and that of others.

If you feel passion for a particular cause or just wish to make a positive impact within your community, there are many resources and groups available to help you do so. For instance, your school may have several service-centered clubs such as Amnesty International, Girl Up, Roots and Shoots, Operation Smile, or Midnight Run. Not only will these clubs offer you the chance to make a positive difference, but they will also enhance your relationships with other students and faculty, build your leadership skills, and advance your societal perspectives. Some schools even allow dedicated students to start and develop their own service-oriented clubs, which is an even greater opportunity for you and like-minded others to pursue your passion and share your talent.

There are also several organizations that you can join outside a school environment, many of which are likely offered by your local community center, religious institution, or library. For example, you may find it rewarding to work in your neighborhood food bank or volunteer at the nearest animal shelter. In addition to opportunities in your own community, there are movements for change at the state and national levels that welcome supportive volunteers and participants. If you aren't sure which programs or causes are out there or which would be particularly meaningful to you, it's helpful to do research online, talk to others who are involved, or try something with a limited commitment so you can assess the time, energy, and engagement that is required to be part of such a group.

Some teenagers, understandably, are looking for ways to embellish their resumes or college applications by claiming to participate in clubs or organizations when they really haven't put in the time or effort. It's best to avoid this practice, as it is disingenuous to fellow participants who wish to truly make a difference, and it reflects a lack of integrity on your part. If you find yourself involved in a club or organization and you aren't able to genuinely commit or do at least the minimum required, explain to those in charge and wish them well in their efforts. Your honesty will be appreciated by all, and you can turn your attention toward helping a different cause or movement that fits better into your life.

Of course, not everyone has the time, skills, or interest to be part of a formal club, organization, or movement for change. You shouldn't feel pressured to join or participate in something your heart isn't on board. Keep in mind that there are meaningful and simple ways that you can contribute as an individual to social and philanthropic causes. For example, you may set a goal of going through your closet at the start of each season and donating any clothing or other useful items that you no longer need to thrift stores and other helpful sites. In fact, there are often seasonal and year-round community drives seeking food, books, toys, hygiene products, and other supplies, and which accept donations from people without being part of an official organization. Other options might include participating in an annual neighborhood clean-up, volunteering weekly or monthly at an animal shelter, or even making a blood donation if you are able.

Whether you are a dedicated member of a school club, a leader of a large movement for societal change, or a quiet and individual contributor for the betterment of others, your efforts will have a rewarding and positive impact on the future. In addition, you will feel gratified in knowing that you have shared your time, talent, and effort to make the world a better place. This will hopefully inspire you to continue to support the causes, movements, and organizations in which you believe so that positive changes will take root and grow.

# THE IMPORTANCE OF FEMALE REPRESENTATION

The representation of women in empowerment and leadership roles is more important than ever. This not only encourages and inspires others to achieve similar goals and positions, but it reflects a more equitable society in which all citizens and groups are valued in their participation and contribution. In addition, positive representation of women in areas like politics, education, the arts, and medicine is associated with greater social and economic opportunities for future generations, regardless of sex or gender.

As a teen girl, it may feel overwhelming to think of your future as a woman and all the potential decisions you'll make involving the pursuit of higher education, careers, relationships, having children, and more. Thankfully, you don't have to make those decisions before you are ready or all at once. There are two important aspects to keep in mind in terms of the roles that you can expect to play as a woman in your lifetime: Women can pursue positions in any field they wish, from careers to motherhood, and women can change their minds. A person's value and capabilities are not and should not be determined or limited by their biological make-up or gender expression, and you should never feel forced into accepting any personal or professional roles — temporarily or permanently — as a girl or woman. In other words, simply because you are a woman doesn't mean that you must become a wife or a mother, and it doesn't mean that you should limit yourself to "traditionally" female professional paths.

Unfortunately, women have faced restrictions in the past, from limited educational and career choices to imposed childbearing and domestic life. In fact, many women across the globe are still faced with difficult circumstances involving oppression, inequality, and discrimination. In some areas, they are prohibited from doing many things, such as accessing healthcare or even leaving their homes, without the permission of a male guardian. This is why universal representation of women as leaders, innovators, and equal participants in society is vital in relation to human rights and individual empowerment.

If there are certain career and/or educational paths that interest you, consider finding women role models and mentors who are currently fulfilling those roles and speak to them about their journeys. Their representation and wisdom will help you to navigate your own path as a woman. In addition, you may find it rewarding as a teen girl to research women of all backgrounds who have been pioneers and activists, paving the way so that you and your peers have greater freedom and more options to reach your goals and dreams. Even discussing the role of women with your mother, grandmother, aunts, and other women in your life can shed light on representation in their generations and their personal feelings about historical, social, cultural, and political advancements that relate to women and your generation.

Ultimately, your life and choices do not and should not need to be defined or restricted by the fact that you are a woman. There is no reason why women of today, regardless of their age and background, shouldn't embrace all potential roles for their futures, whether they follow a more traditional path or blaze a new trail. This includes pursuing higher education, careers, hobbies, relationships, motherhood, and all other life experiences. Your skills, talents, and abilities as a person will empower you to accomplish your goals and fulfill your dreams, whatever they may be.

# CHAPTER EIGHT: DIGITAL LIFE AND ONLINE ETIQUETTE

People are spending more time than ever on their electronic devices, and teenage girls are no exception. This has led to what many consider a "digital life," in which a significant part of our daily existence and personal identity is spent and formed online. For example, you may be part of online groups such as gaming communities, social media platforms, and discussion forums where you spend time participating in activities and interacting with others in the same digital space. Though you may not have met all (or any) of your online connections in person, you may consider them friends or at least important parts of your digital community. You may also consider your online activities to be part of your personal and/or professional journey toward adulthood, lending validity and importance to your digital life.

Of course, though the time you spend and the relationships you form in your digital life are valuable and have their advantages, it's essential to keep in mind that your non-digital life is even more important and precious. There really is no substitute for in-person, human connection. Unfortunately, many people develop behaviors similar to addiction when it comes to the overuse of digital technology, whether it's preoccupation with online gaming or constant checking of social media. The effects of this can be detrimental to your mental and physical health in addition to harming your personal relationships, academic progress, and professional success. Ideally, you should keep a proper, healthy balance between your digital life and actual life. This may include setting strict limits for the amount of time you spend in the digital world and the hours during which you are online. Ultimately, your actual (non-digital) activities, relationships, identity, and existence should always take priority over and never be compromised by any part of your digital life.

Additionally, just as you would hold yourself to a code of conduct or etiquette in your non-digital life, online etiquette is an important tool for your digital life. Etiquette, in general, reflects a consensus among certain groups or societies of what is considered proper or customary behavior. For example, practicing good table manners while eating is a typical standard of etiquette in most public places as well as in your own home. Though being online may feel like an anonymous or solitary experience, the digital world is also made up of groups and communities in which there are expectations of etiquette. In fact, the term often used to refer to online etiquette is "netiquette," a combination of internet and etiquette.

Overall, netiquette involves common sense and mannerly behavior, just as etiquette does in the non-digital world. This means being respectful and considerate of others, both in tone and words. Keep in mind that what you post online, whether it's a comment, discussion response, or observation, is likely to be read by a wider audience than you expect and to remain online for a long time. In addition, online communication lacks the subtleties that can be conveyed through body language, facial expression, and tone of voice, increasing the likelihood of misinterpretation or misunderstanding. Therefore, if you wouldn't say something in a public or professional setting, then it's best to avoid saying it within any digital format or platform.

# RESPONSIBLE SOCIAL MEDIA USE

If you have grown up using social media, you may feel that you are already aware of how to do it safely and responsibly. This is likely true, but it's important to be reminded of ways to protect yourself from any danger or negative outcomes that can result from unsafe or irresponsible social media use. For example, overuse and constant checking of social media can have negative effects on your health and well-being. This includes platforms such as Facebook, Instagram, TikTok, and the many other online community sites in which you may participate. Therefore, it's important to be responsible for your content and limit your time and presence on these platforms so you don't develop unhealthy habits or unsafe behavioral patterns.

In addition, it's wise to keep in mind that your social media activity has the potential to affect your personal reputation and professional opportunities — now and in the future. This means that any irresponsible posts you make, or pictures you share can have direct consequences and implications on your life's paths and goals. Though this may seem unfair in the sense that you should be entitled to freely express your individuality within what appears to be a closed or limited audience of followers, the truth is that social media sites and their content are understood to be public, not private. The groups and individuals you associate with on social media can also impact your digital and non-digital life. For its many benefits, social media is much like a permanent, public record of your words, actions, and relationships — all of which can unfortunately be taken out of context and create obstacles for your future success.

Perhaps the greatest threat to your safety when using social media involves your personal identifiable information or PII. PII is all the data that is specifically associated with your identity as a person, such as your full name, address, phone number, Social Security number, birth date, and bank account information. If someone gets ahold of your PII, they can potentially compromise your identity through theft or fraud. This can lead to serious legal, financial, personal, and professional issues and consequences that can take years to fix. Even worse, the more someone knows about you as an individual, the more exposed you are to being harmed. The best and only way to preserve your health, safety, and the security of your identity is to never post, share, or give out any personal information of any kind. If you do not want the public to know something about you, then it's essential to keep it private and completely away from social media.

Another thing to keep in mind is that not everyone on social media is who they portray themselves to be. Unfortunately, these platforms and sites are full of scammers, imposters, and individuals with even more dangerous intentions. Not only are these bad actors present on social media, but many of them are incredibly practiced and savvy in what they do. Often, their victims don't realize they've been harmed or taken advantage of until too late. To keep yourself safe, do not accept any "friend" requests or connections from people you do not know. Keep your settings as "private" as each social media platform allows, and you should absolutely refuse, report, and block anyone who demands or solicits money, pictures, meeting in person, or personal information of any kind. If you have uncomfortable feelings or doubts about someone or something involving your social media, let a trusted adult know immediately before the situation gets out of hand.

Though social media certainly has its negative and even potentially dangerous sides, it can be a positive experience for those who wish to participate in a smart and healthy way. For the most part, these platforms allow people to connect and stay in touch with others, enjoy similar interests, and share information. However, just as you would be responsible and protect your personal safety offline, it's even more essential to do so when using online platforms. Once again, if you are ever unsure or uncomfortable about something or someone related to social media, let a trusted adult or person of authority know right away. They can help you protect your safety and security.

# NAVIGATING ONLINE FRIENDSHIPS

These days, it's not unusual to have several individual and groups of online friendships with people from diverse backgrounds all over the world, many that would have been impossible to form before the internet. Online relationships also allow us to stay in close touch with distant relatives and friends who have relocated, as well as to meet new people through social media and other platforms. However, just like in "real life," it's important to consider how to navigate online friendships in a healthy manner and avoid potential pitfalls and problems.

You may know some adults who don't really understand online friendships. They may be under the impression that a friend is someone who you must meet and interact with in person. However, online friendships are both legitimate and valuable in most cases. They are usually based on shared, often very specific interests, and such relationships may not be easy to find otherwise in the offline world. In addition, online friendships can essentially provide many of the same benefits as non-digital relationships, such as companionship, exchange of knowledge, empathy, and lots of fun.

Though online friendships offer similar benefits, they can be more challenging to navigate than in-person relationships. For example, miscommunication may be more likely to happen due to geographical, language, or cultural differences. To avoid this, remember to treat your online friends with consideration and respect in addition to being open-minded toward their beliefs and values. You may also find it difficult to devote consistent attention and effort toward your digital life when your non-digital life becomes busy or requires more focus. Thankfully, these pitfalls and problems are usually temporary and can be overcome the more you get to know your online friends. Perhaps the biggest challenge with online friendships is the fact that, unless you are lucky enough to be able to meet in person, they don't always tend to grow and evolve at the same pace or in the same ways as offline friendships. In other words, your interests and commitments are likely to change as you get older and experience more things, which can potentially make it harder to maintain your relationships with online friends.

Ultimately, most experts agree that online friendships should not overshadow or be at the expense of in-person friendships. Both types of friends are important for creating social bonds and emotional connections that enhance your quality of life and prevent feelings of isolation and loneliness. Yet in-person friends allow us to practice interpersonal skills, learn social-emotional cues through body language and facial expression, and communicate in meaningful ways that are otherwise limited when we are online. Therefore, it's essential to balance the time and energy you invest in online friendships with those that you have formed outside the digital world.

# BUILDING A POSITIVE DIGITAL FOOTPRINT

Though it has negative connotations in some ways, your digital life can be a positive force now and in the future. Social media and online platforms are unprecedented and instrumental in allowing us to connect with people across the globe. The internet offers an astonishing amount of information and inspiration, opportunities to research almost any subject, and ways to develop innumerable skill sets as well. With so much at our fingertips, we can create a foundation for lifelong learning and betterment in addition to building a positive digital footprint with careful attention to avoiding long-term mistakes and consequences.

A digital footprint is a phrase used to describe someone's activity online. It may surprise and disturb some people to know that pretty much all actions online can be digitally traced. This is especially true if the data is public, such as anything put on social media, and therefore easily gathered. You might be aware that your online activity can be accessed and followed by advertisers and marketers, internet providers, and data companies. However, it can also be visible to potential employers, college admissions personnel, hackers, and even cyber-criminals. This can lead to negative outcomes such as someone accessing and using your information to pose as you, perpetrating fraud, or stealing your identity — and these are problems that can take a long time to fix.

Even if your information and data are not stolen or used for negative purposes, your digital footprint can greatly influence and harm your online reputation. For example, let's say that you are angry with a classmate and decide to post something hurtful about them on social media in a moment of distraction. Though you may forget all about it, that post may be seen someday by a person in charge of hiring for a job you want or someone making decisions among college applicants. It may not seem fair, but your online speech, photos, and activity are all a reflection of who you are to those you haven't met in person.

Thankfully, there are ways to avoid or at least minimize your risk when it comes to your digital footprint so that you can create a positive online reputation. Obviously, you should never take part in or post photos, as well as any other online evidence of criminal activity such as underage drinking, drug use, etc. You should also avoid any participation in or association with online bullying in addition to affiliation with any hate groups. Keep in mind as well that digitally sharing any suggestive or inappropriate material is equivalent to sharing it with the public. One way to keep your online behavior and activity in check is to imagine someone you admire and respect looking over your shoulder every minute that you are active. This will ensure that you build as positive an online footprint as possible.

You may be under the impression that images, text, videos, etc., can be deleted or removed from the internet. This may be possible in some cases, but it doesn't account for what others may have shared, saved, or made available somewhere else. You may also count on the idea that any online "mistakes" or behaviors would be considered personal, private, or irrelevant in terms of employment or impacting other significant opportunities, yet the risk is quite high that any negative online perception will affect your personal reputation, integrity, and future—fair or not. So don't be fooled by the anonymous feeling that digital devices appear to offer and remember that anything you do or say online is essentially on public display. Today, it is easy to find online tutorials walking you through how to ensure your privacy on all of your accounts. If you have not done this or have not done it in a while, it might be a good idea to walk through and "clean house" in terms of your online presence.

# CHAPTER NINE: BODY IMAGE AND SELF-CARE

Since you know the significant changes that your body will go through in the teen years, it's vital to have a strong foundation for a healthy body image and how to care for your physical well-being. Body image is a complex concept that centers around what we think and how we feel about our physical selves. Body image is complex because it is not a fixed state of mind — you may have alternating positive and negative feelings (or both) about the way you look from moment to moment as well as over time. In addition, body image is based on *perception*, not reality. In other words, what you "see" and believe to be true about your physical self is a representation and not an exact depiction.

For example, even when we look in the mirror, we are not viewing ourselves as others actually see us. That's because the mirror shows us a reverse image and is additionally affected by light, movement, angles, and other factors. This is also the reason why you might be surprised by how you look in a photograph (which is not a reverse image) compared to how you look in a mirror. The point is that our body image is made up of "versions" of our physical selves that we combine and store in our thoughts but that don't exist in reality. The more we scrutinize, compare, and/or devalue the perception of our bodies, the more negative our self-worth can become, which can seriously threaten our physical, emotional, and mental health.

Of course, most people want to be happy and proud of their physical appearance, so they feel attractive or that they fit in with what society considers "normal." However, preoccupation with the way you appear on the outside is a disservice to your mind, body, and who you are as a person. It's far healthier and more beneficial to balance the time and energy you may spend on looking attractive with appreciating your physical well-being and caring for your body to protect your future health. This doesn't mean that you won't have moments or days during which you feel sluggish, unattractive, or insecure about your body image, but it does mean that you will have the ability to recognize that these feelings are temporary and they can be put into perspective in consideration of the many wonderful ways your body functions each day and the more important goals to focus on in your lifetime.

Ultimately, it makes sense that we've all got pretty much the same parts on the inside and just different packaging on the outside, though this is easy to forget. Whereas you may look at someone's curly hair as beautiful, they may be wishing for longer legs like you have. Genetics and biology don't offer us a menu of physical traits from which to choose—and that's a good thing. The challenge is to prioritize and value the person you are rather than the way you look, despite all the internal and external messages that your physical appearance should change or improve. This involves learning how to separate your body image from your self-image, being thankful for your body as it grows and changes, appreciating physical diversity among others, and caring for your long-term physical health.

# CELEBRATING BODY DIVERSITY

Many people trace problems with body image and self-esteem among teenagers to how the media portrays "perfection" and shapes the definition of physical beauty, both socially and culturally. This is rightly so on several levels; the media is significantly influential in terms of what ends up being considered the standard for body size, shape, and other aesthetics. Unfortunately, these standards rarely reflect the way actual people look. They are also unattainable and next to impossible to achieve due to manufactured settings, lighting, camera angles, and digital alterations that determine what we see in media images. Yet we consistently buy and consume this imagery (literally and figuratively) rather than acknowledge and call attention to its false, fictitious nature. As a result, the effects of these media stereotypes and lack of physical diversity can erode the self-esteem and self-confidence of anyone who doesn't meet such fabricated standards — especially impressionable and self-conscious teens.

Thankfully, there are some movements toward supporting healthy body image and portraying greater physical diversity in certain forms of media. However, we still have a long way to go in overcoming pervasive social and cultural impressions of what is attractive so that inclusivity is prioritized more than exclusivity. Celebrating body diversity is one important way to support more realistic and encompassing beauty standards. There are many things you can do to celebrate and promote body diversity, not the least of which is embracing a healthy body image for yourself rather than aspiring to look like or comparing yourself to media stereotypes. Body diversity and positivity movements also emphasize overall physical health and wellness rather than a focus on body size and shape. You can support this by shifting compliments toward character traits such as generosity, intelligence, and empathy instead of physical attributes or appearances. Even more important is avoiding and condemning any semblance of body shaming, discrimination, or criticism, whether among your friends, family members, or social media followers.

Directly combating media stereotypes that undermine body diversity may seem beyond your scope as an individual teen girl. However, there are ways to achieve this as it pertains to your life and choices. Of course, one of the first steps is to recognize media portrayals and marketing campaigns for what they are: brand and product sales. Corporations invest a great deal, so consumers feel pressured or tempted to buy products, often without even realizing they've been targeted. Another is to resist these persuasive sales tactics and remain true to your authentic self. Following diverse groups and individuals on social media is another way to challenge online stereotypes and promote acceptance. Ultimately, the more educated and socially aware you become in relation to physical diversity, body positivity, and negative media influences, the easier it will be for you to personally challenge stereotypes and support others in doing so.

Just taking a moment to imagine the stress, money, time, and energy that could be saved by people embracing physical health rather than attempting to reach unrealistic beauty standards is staggering—and these beauty "investments" are heavily directed toward women despite the frequent economic disadvantages they already face. Society would be much more productive, and people would probably be much more content if we valued diversity and prioritized inclusivity as well as acceptance and support of ourselves and others. Unattainable media stereotypes will only persist as long as they remain unchallenged and unexposed and as long as people continue to chase them.

# SELF-CARE RITUALS AND ROUTINES

One of the most important principles you can learn as a teen girl is the importance of taking care of yourself. Practicing self-care rituals and routines will get you in the habit of ensuring that your health and well-being are attended to and maintained each day while you are a teenager and in the future. As our schedules become busy with school, work, hobbies, friends, and other commitments, it can be a challenge to find time for self-care. For example, you may feel too rushed during the day to regularly drink water for hydration, or you may shortchange yourself of an hour or two of sleep to catch up on homework or social media. However, the earlier you prioritize healthy rituals and routines, the more integrated they will be in your daily life.

Many self-care rituals and routines are centered around personal hygiene. This would include caring for your body, skin, teeth, and hair with daily bathing and washing, moisturizing, applying sunscreen, etc. This is important for social reasons but primarily for your sense of wellness and self-confidence. Most people address their personal hygiene when they get up and before they go to bed. However, if taking a bath or shower relaxes you or you enjoy experimenting with different makeup trends, any time of day is good for self-care. One trap to avoid is the aggressive marketing that comes with personal care brands and makeup. Such advertising can make you feel that you "must" buy certain items for your health and beauty, which can leave you with a lot less money and a lot of unnecessary products. It's far better to choose the basics and whatever you are comfortable using, search for good reviews, and purchase only what you need and can afford.

In addition to your outer body, it's essential to establish self-care rituals and routines for your inner physical health as well. One of the best routines you can set for your overall well-being is daily hydration. Most experts recommend drinking between six to eight glasses of plain water each day. Other beverages and certain foods provide hydration as well, but water is truly the healthiest choice for your body. You can set up a general routine to drink a glass of water every one to two hours during the day and allow for more water consumption on days when it is particularly warm, dry, or when you have participated in more physical activity than usual. Overall, it's important to pay attention to any feelings of thirst, which might mean that your body's fluid levels are low. So, at the first sign of feeling thirsty, be sure to drink some water as soon as possible.

It's also wise to set daily routines for healthy eating. This might include three basic meals (breakfast, lunch, and dinner) as well as a couple of smart snacks in between. Of course, common knowledge is that your diet should consist of plenty of fruits, vegetables, lean protein, and whole grains, and a limited amount of sugar, fried foods, and caffeine. Remember that you don't have to be perfect as far as what you eat—just try to keep a healthy balance when possible and make wise choices overall. A regular exercise routine will also help you maintain your body's health and fitness. This can involve anything from sports practices and conditioning to taking brisk walks or doing yoga on your own. To make sure that you recover properly from daily activities and to protect your well-being, don't forget to make sleep a priority as well. A consistent bedtime ritual that includes zero screen time and relaxation techniques can ensure that you develop healthy sleep patterns and habits.

One essential aspect of self-care that some people forget is to schedule an annual medical wellness exam. This allows your doctor or other medical professional to establish certain baselines while you are healthy for future comparison and to ensure that you aren't currently facing any health risks or issues. Yearly check-ups also give you the chance to grow comfortable in prioritizing and discussing your physical and mental health. These appointments offer the opportunity to ask questions about your body and address any other health concerns that may be on your mind, especially if you are experiencing any signs of anxiety, depression, etc. Your medical care provider can recommend necessary treatments and/or supportive services to improve and maintain your total wellness. Overall, it's important to remember that there is nothing more valuable than caring for your health, and the sooner you implement routines and rituals to support your well-being, the more likely you are to continue them in the future.

# EMBRACING
# BODY CHANGES

Our bodies go through changes throughout our entire lives. We grow taller in our youth and then often shrink in height in our older age. Baby teeth fall out and are replaced by permanent ones. Hair appears and sometimes disappears in certain areas, and it changes color. We can gain and lose weight, muscle, bone density, coordination, and balance. Our skin cells actually regenerate each month, on average, on top of the changes that come with possible scars, oily pores, dryness, freckles, pimples, and more. Essentially, nothing about our physical appearance remains the same, whether we like it or not, and that's just the outside of the body. The internal physical changes we experience are even more numerous and astounding.

Of course, the physical changes that teen girls typically undergo during puberty are quite significant on the inside and outside. These changes can also be surprising if you aren't prepared for what to expect, from developing breasts to growing pubic hair to starting menstruation. Understandably, some girls (and even grown women) feel a bit of awkwardness or discomfort when discussing such physical developments. In addition, it is important to note the unfortunate and unfair tendency within many societies to sexualize (put in a sexual context) the female body as it matures, as this can definitely be a factor in influencing how teen girls understand and embrace their changing physicality. However, these changes are the body's natural way of maturing into womanhood and preparing for reproduction, and there is never a reason for them to be associated with shame or embarrassment.

The onset of menstruation, more typically known as getting your period, can be a meaningful milestone on the path to womanhood.

Yet, at first, dealing with your period is usually an adjustment. For example, you may not get it monthly or with any regularity for a year or longer. In addition, your period may be accompanied by cramps, mood swings, and other symptoms. Therefore, it's important to be patient with yourself as you learn which methods and products work best for you to handle your cycle. If you are concerned about any aspect of your period, whether it's blood flow, soreness, heightened emotions, or something else., be sure to talk to a trusted female family member or friend who perhaps has more experience. It's also essential that you let your doctor or other medical professional know that you have begun menstruation so they can help you navigate any health issues in addition to answering your questions. Be sure to keep track of the first day of bleeding, how many days it lasts, and how heavy your period is during each cycle. This way, you'll have the information available when you need it and a record in case you face any significant changes.

Most people understand and expect physical changes to their bodies as they get older; it's the lack of acceptance and appreciation of such changes that often presents challenges, produces resistance, and potentially results in negative emotions and behaviors. Teen girls, unfortunately, can experience great difficulty when it comes to embracing how their bodies change with the onset of puberty and womanhood—especially if they view female representation in the media as the standard. Whether this difficulty leads to mild dissatisfaction, prolonged insecurity, or harsh self-criticism, the outcome can range from slightly debilitating to intensely harmful in terms of self-esteem and self-perception.

The key is to recognize and avoid the confusion of body image (what you think and feel about your physical self) with self-image (your perception of all the characteristics and capabilities that make up who you are as an individual). Just as a car is more than its shape and paint color, you are much more than your physical appearance. And just as you wouldn't base the worth of a car just on how it looks from the outside, your sense of self and who you are should never be based on or associated with how you look—especially since the human body goes through so many physical changes anyway. Instead, the source of your self-worth should be the way you treat others, the way you treat yourself, and all the numerous gifts, strengths, and talents you have to share with the world. This includes your physical health and your body's incredible capacity to function and accomplish so much each day.

One effective way to embrace the wonder of your body and all its changes is to practice daily mindfulness. There are many mindfulness exercises that are related to meditation, including taking a quiet moment to focus on your present surroundings, your five physical senses, and your breathing. Body mindfulness can also be practiced through relaxation and paying attention to your body parts, from top to bottom, as well as the way you think and feel about each part. Concentrating on your overall physical being and your relationship to its individual parts will allow you to appreciate the human body's intricate connections and ability to function.

Not only does mindfulness allow you a specific amount of time each day to be present, calm, and self-aware, but it also gives you the opportunity to notice your physical wellness as part of your self-care routine. This can directly lead to gratitude for all that your body does and can do. There are many people who suffer from physical complications, injuries, illnesses, disabilities, and other debilitating conditions that would be difficult for those with healthy bodies to even imagine. Though the physical changes associated with the teen years can feel awkward and uncomfortable at times, those feelings are almost always temporary. It's far more beneficial to embrace the changes that come along with growing into adulthood and focus instead on taking good care of your body and being grateful for the physical health you have while you have it.

# CHAPTER 10: FINANCES AND INDEPENDENCE

A big part of adulthood is expanding your financial knowledge and independence so you can support yourself and be economically responsible. Unfortunately, practical money management and basic financial literacy are rarely taught in school settings. In addition, for many families and cultures, the subjects of money and finance are somewhat uncomfortable and might be considered impolite to discuss openly. This can make for a steep financial learning curve in the teen years and early adulthood, as well as make it more difficult to avoid stress and mistakes in money matters.

Thankfully, you can be proactive in learning about finances to prepare for becoming independent. This doesn't mean that you need to follow the stock market or understand international political economics. Instead, you can focus on learning to manage money through budgeting, saving, and other strategies, in addition to considering various options related to post-high school education and how to pay for it. Getting actual work experience through a part-time job or internship is another important means of understanding money matters on your way to attaining financial growth and independence.

One important financial lesson that can make a big difference in your life as a teen is understanding the difference between spending on what you *need* and what you *want*. It's no secret that we live in a consumer-based society, and for the most part we don't even need to leave the house to do the majority of our shopping. This low-effort, immediate gratification system certainly has its advantages. However, the downside is that, as buyers, our decisions often require very little careful consideration or critical thought in terms of what we purchase. Not only does this result in the accumulation of a lot of unnecessary items, but it also makes it difficult to track whether we are spending money out of necessity or something else, such as boredom, advertising pressure, etc. Of course, it's natural to spend money when we have it and to occasionally spend it frivolously. The key is to do so in a mindful, intentional way and acknowledge why you are making the purchase. In this way, if you notice that you are spending more money on things "just because," you can change your habits to support better financial strategies for the future, such as budgeting, saving, or even just setting a waiting period to see if you still want to make the purchase when the moment has passed.

It can be scary and stressful to think about the complex process of choosing a career, getting hired for full-time employment, and making enough money to live and thrive on your own as an adult. Keep in mind, though, that you have many years to make those decisions, gain experience, become qualified, and take action. In addition, there are many sources of guidance and support to help you on your journey toward financial independence and future success. Thankfully, the more you learn about making, spending, and saving money as a teen girl, the more opportunities and knowledge you'll have to make wise money decisions along the path to adulthood.

# BUDGETING, SAVING, AND FINANCIAL LITERACY

Financial literacy refers to a general understanding of money and how to manage it. Of course, this is an essential part of adulthood when it comes to employment, paying for expenses, avoiding debt, and making investments. As a teen, it's more likely that your parent(s) or guardian(s) have the financial responsibility of running and maintaining the household, such as paying for utilities, rent or mortgage, groceries, and so on. However, learning the basics of budgeting, saving, and financial literacy is important before you become financially independent to ensure a successful future.

In a sense, budgeting comes down to addition and subtraction, or money earned and money spent. Most teens have a limited income because they are not expected to work full-time while in school. However, many teens also earn some money from various sources, whether through part-time work, occasional jobs like babysitting, doing household chores, or monetary gifts. Often, this money is considered "disposable" income, in the sense that you can probably do what you'd like with it and are likely to spend it. Creating a budget with this disposable income is an excellent way to practice managing your money so that you spend and save responsibly when you are older. For example, if you are interested in buying a new video game but don't have enough money yet to do so, you can create a budget to help you reach that goal. Essentially, you would list your earnings (money you have available) and your expenses (cost of the video game and any other known expenses). This budget will give you a clear idea of how much you need to earn and/or save to purchase the game.

Saving is another important aspect of financial literacy. Unfortunately, consumerism (buying goods and services) is heavily emphasized in many parts of our society, so having the self-discipline to save money can be challenging. The problem with not developing a habit of saving is that you are less likely to have the necessary financial resources in a future emergency. For example, if your car breaks down and costs more money to repair than what you have saved, you may be without transportation for a significant time. Most experts recommend putting 10–20 percent of your earnings into savings right away. For instance, if you have thoughtful and generous grandparents who send you 20 dollars a month, you should put two to four of those dollars in your savings each time. In a year, you would have 24-48 dollars set aside. This is an excellent way to not only build an emergency fund but also set limitations on your spending so that you make more thoughtful decisions with your money.

It can take time and patience to learn the importance of financial literacy, but the sooner you start, the smarter you'll be when it comes to managing money. Working with a budget and developing a habit of saving as early as possible can help you avoid some of the stressful and complex financial pitfalls that many face in adulthood, such as accumulating debt, lack of an emergency fund, or relying heavily on credit. In addition, you'll have a greater understanding of money as a resource and how to use it thoughtfully and wisely.

# PREPARING FOR COLLEGE

Many people view a college degree as an important step toward a solid career and financial independence. However, preparing for college can feel like scaling a huge mountain for teenagers. There is tremendous pressure early on to succeed and excel in academics, sports, extracurricular activities, work experience, community service, and more to create a well-rounded profile that is distinguishable among thousands of others vying for the same admission slots. In addition to this overwhelming sense of competition, there are the added hurdles of application deadlines, writing essays, taking standardized tests, getting letters of recommendation, applying for scholarships, and other logistical matters associated with just getting accepted to a school of your choice — none of which actually prepares you for attending and succeeding in college once you get there.

Though college preparation can be extremely stressful, thankfully, there are resources available to provide you with information and support. High school guidance counselors can help you through the application process, organize a plan to complete required tasks and meet established deadlines. There are also educational websites that offer helpful tips, including how to set up college campus tours for those schools you are considering. Finding and applying for scholarships and other financial aid sources to help with the expense of earning a degree is a large part of college preparation, in addition to the application process. Though this takes a great deal of attention, dedication, and effort, accumulating scholarship money and other financial aid can help offset the need for student loans, which can be a long-term financial burden. Guidance counselors at the high school and college level, as well as online searches, can also assist with finding scholarships and applying for financial aid.

Even deciding where, when, or if you'd like to go to college at all can be challenging. Many teens choose to take the relatively traditional path of graduating from high school and then attending a four-year college or university to earn a bachelor's degree. There are many benefits to this, including the personal, educational, and professional opportunities that come with such an experience, the good fortune to meet people from different regions and backgrounds, and the chance to grow independently and pursue future goals. However, college is expensive and can have other drawbacks for those who aren't fully ready or truly interested in going. In fact, there is so much emphasis on receiving acceptance and being admitted that the bulk of the preparation for successfully navigating college once you're there is often overshadowed and overlooked. It can feel overwhelming to suddenly live away from home and be responsible for managing your schedule, resources, and personal well-being, all while facing the academic pressures of higher education. This can result in setbacks that range from participating in high-risk behaviors to feelings of isolation and low self-esteem to academic probation and other consequences.

Therefore, it's important to consider the many other options for high school graduates that can be just as rewarding and beneficial as a four-year college program. For example, community colleges typically offer two-year associate degree programs with more flexibility and less cost. This is an excellent path for those who wish to complete general education college courses while working or deciding on a specific area of study and then potentially transfer to a four-year university to earn a bachelor's degree. Trade and vocational schools provide specialized training and field experience for those interested in certain careers that do not require a four-year degree. Many colleges offer online and/or self-paced courses for students who wish to live at home or away from expensive campus housing. Some people may decide to join a branch of the armed forces to earn money, experience, and future educational benefits through the GI Bill. Others may choose to take a "gap" year away from formal education to get job experience, perform service missions, travel, or develop important life skills.

No matter which path you choose, you will find opportunities for learning, experience, and broadening your worldview — and you can always change your course and your mind. Though earning a college degree can definitely help you reach career goals and expand future opportunities, it is not the only way to achieve financial independence. In fact, most people go through numerous changes as they navigate their financial lives, including switching jobs, earning advanced degrees, making investments, etc. Therefore, it's important to look at and prepare for college (if that's your preference) as a holistic experience of individual growth and freedom as well as potential economic advancement. And don't forget that there are many other options and paths you can take to prepare for adulthood and financial freedom.

# YOUR FIRST JOBS
# AND INTERNSHIPS

In the past few years, the rate of teen employment has dropped significantly. This includes part-time jobs during both the school year and summer months. There are many likely explanations why fewer teens than ever are choosing not to get work experience, such as putting focus on academics, being overscheduled with extracurricular activities, or simply having no interest in part-time jobs that are available. However, this decision to stay out of the workforce may be shortsighted for many reasons as well. Getting your first job as a teenager can be an extremely valuable experience in terms of making money, learning practical skills and time management, developing interpersonal skills and relationships, and being responsible to others.

There are many options when it comes to getting your first job as a teen. Most places of business have an age requirement of 15 or 16 for hiring, but many rely on young workers to fill part-time positions after school, on weekends, and during school vacation months. If you are interested in getting a formal part-time job, you might consider your local movie theaters, coffee shops, restaurants, retail stores, grocery stores, etc. Though these jobs may not appear glamorous, they provide the opportunity to make a steady wage and interact with all types of people. In addition, showing that you can commit to a job as well as school and other activities is an excellent way to stand out among other college applicants and to future employers. There are many helpful approaches to getting hired and navigating your first job. You can check local "help wanted" ads or signs to find out who is hiring and then submit your job application. You may also check job boards posted at your school or community center for ideas. Once you have applied, the next step would be to wait for a job interview. Your parents, guidance counselors, and other trusted adults can give you many tips for successfully getting and keeping your first job.

If you'd rather not have a formal part-time job, there are many opportunities for entrepreneurship as a way to earn money and work experience. This essentially means running your own business to provide goods or services. For example, you can offer tutoring, babysitting, pet-sitting, and other helpful tasks at the convenience of your schedule and at a reasonable rate of pay. Of course, you should ensure that you have the proper qualifications, knowledge, and experience to provide such services. To get started, you can advertise your skills and availability on social media, through neighbors, friends, and family members, or in local publications. Often, if your customers are happy with your abilities and work ethic, they will refer you to others through word-of-mouth and recommendations so that your reputation and entrepreneurial skills will grow.

Internships are another important source of work experience for teens. An internship is a position in a specific field of employment or education that provides direct learning, skill-building, and experience. Like a formal job, internships usually require an application and interview process. Though not all interns are paid for their work, they gain valuable benefits in terms of expertise and networking with others who are established in the desired career or educational field. For example, you may be considering veterinary science as a future career and decide to seek out an intern position with your local vet. This would be a valuable opportunity to "shadow" and learn from an expert directly about what the job entails on a daily basis, which skills are essential, and whether such a career is a realistic and suitable fit for you. Working as an intern would also provide the chance for you to perform helpful tasks and gain some hands-on experience. If you are interested in trying an internship, your school guidance counselor is a good resource for information, or you could reach out and express your intentions to local businesses and professionals.

First jobs, internships, and entrepreneurship are valuable avenues to pursue as a teen if you are able and willing. Of course, it may seem challenging to add yet another obligation to your already full schedule. However, no other experience will prepare you as well for the responsibility of employment or offer as many real-world learning and earning opportunities. Though working takes commitment, time, and effort, the results are usually very rewarding. Even a weekend or summer position will offer many benefits in the short and long term as you meet new people and learn new skills.

# CHAPTER ELEVEN: HOBBIES, TALENTS, AND PERSONAL GROWTH

As we get older, we tend to prioritize things like work, school, relationships, and other commitments more so than our hobbies, talents, and activities that support our personal growth. This makes sense, considering how busy our schedules tend to get and how many people, events, and projects compete for our attention. However, discovering and pursuing meaningful pastimes is often what makes our lives enjoyable and valuable. Therefore, it's important to set aside time and dedication for personal fulfillment, beginning in your teen years and carrying through to adulthood.

Many people turn to hobbies as a way to relax, interact with others, pursue creativity, and enjoy specific interests. A hobby is something that you do in your free time because you find the experience likable and rewarding. Hobbies can be enjoyed individually or as a group, indoors or outdoors, and regularly or occasionally. Some people choose hobbies that are useful and productive as well as meaningful, such as cooking, gardening, or learning languages. Others may prefer hobbies that are more leisurely and informal, such as reading, painting, or doing puzzles.

If you aren't sure which hobbies would be beneficial or engaging for you, take a few moments to consider what you find interesting, calming, fun, and fulfilling. If you feel rewarded when participating in group or community activities, you might take up membership in a book or cycling club. If you have a special interest in artistic activities, you might consider photography, creative writing, or drawing. No matter what you choose as a hobby, you'll find that having an enjoyable activity to pursue in your free time is good for your overall health, personal growth, and long-term happiness.

Discovering and developing your talents is another meaningful way to grow as a person. Most people associate talent with being famous, unique, or successful, such as a star athlete or celebrated performer. However, you don't need to reach a certain level of expertise or achievement to have talent. Essentially, anything for which you have a natural ability or special skill is a talent. For example, you might be naturally gifted when it comes to singing, writing, or running. Some people have inherent skills when it comes to public speaking, caring for animals, or even organizing closets and other spaces. Of course, talent isn't simply something that a person is good at doing. There is also a component of energy and enthusiasm that comes along with being talented at something. This is what makes it personally rewarding, meaningful, and enjoyable.

During the teen years, especially for girls, a lot of focus is put on understanding and coping with physical changes, growth, and development. Yet this time is also one for growing as an individual and finding out what makes you unique, special, and fulfilled. As you explore different interests, you will become open to new ideas, connect with other people, and learn about yourself. By discovering your hobbies, talents, passions, and other creative methods of self-expression as a teen, you will establish a healthy balance between tasks that you must do and activities that you wish to do. This will have long-term benefits as you grow into adulthood and become the person you are meant to be.

# DISCOVERING NEW PASSIONS

As a teen girl, you are likely to spend much of your time focusing on building your future through academics, internships, sports, volunteer work, clubs, and other experiences to ensure your successful transition into adulthood. Though these activities and commitments will definitely keep you busy, it's also important to discover new passions and develop your natural skills. This will allow you to maintain a healthy balance between what you must do and what you truly enjoy doing. You may even find that your passions and skills will lead you to rewarding career opportunities and/or lifelong friendships.

Most people define a passion as something that creates strong emotion, inspires dedication, and provides fulfillment. You may have several passions that range across many subjects and/or activities, and these passions may change or evolve over time. For example, you may be passionate about caring for animals, which could lead to a lifetime commitment of advocating for animal rights or volunteering at shelters. You may also discover a passion for reading a certain genre when you are exposed to it in an English or history class and be inspired to study it further in college. Some people have a passion for playing sports, creating art, working to better their community, or playing an instrument—the possibilities are nearly endless. When you find an activity or subject that captivates, energizes, and inspires you, then you have likely found one of your passions.

One of the most important ways to discover new passions is to keep an open mind. The more open you are to new experiences, concepts, and people, the more likely you are to find what brings you joy and excitement. In turn, you will have the opportunity to hone and apply your natural skills as you grow more dedicated to your passions. Honing your skills means sharpening and improving them. For example, if you discover a passion for baking, you will probably be inspired to try different recipes, ingredients, and techniques. By doing so, your baking skills will expand and become more refined. This relationship between passions and skills creates an innovative and rewarding cycle that will continue to grow.

Remember that you are much more than the list of achievements, activities, scores, and positions that are included on your college

116

application or job resume. Part of what brings meaning to life and humanity is discovering and pursuing our passions outside of what is expected of us in our everyday lives. This also allows us to learn and develop skills that facilitate our future success and enjoyment beyond school, work, and other daily commitments. Finding what makes us feel passionate keeps us inspired and enhances our lifelong personal growth.

# CREATIVITY AND SELF-EXPRESSION

One of the strongest methods of developing and supporting your personal growth is to understand the power of journaling, creativity, and other means of self-expression. Humans are unique in their individuality, and creation is a natural and healthy outlet for conveying our thoughts and feelings, whether privately or publicly. There are many ways to express yourself through creativity, such as writing/journaling, music, dance, dramatic arts, painting, or sculpting. Finding the best creative methods of expressing yourself can be a powerful part of your journey into adulthood and provide you with mental, emotional, and physical health benefits.

Some people mistake journaling for keeping a daily account of activities, events, and experiences — which is actually more of how a diary is used. True journaling is the process of expressing your deep and personal thoughts, feelings, and ideas through writing (or typing). The act of doing this can help put things into perspective, bring you clarity, and offer a greater understanding of your inner self. In turn, keeping a journal can reduce your stress and anxiety while also enhancing your creative thinking and problem-solving skills. Most people consider journaling to be a private activity, meaning that their words are not intended to be read by anyone else. This is helpful, as it allows you to express yourself in an unfiltered and truthful way.

Even if you have never considered journaling before, it's an easy process to start. There are formal journals for purchase that are already set up for you to respond to daily quotes or questions, or you can just use blank paper to write down what is on your mind and in your heart. If you have trouble getting started, one strategy is to keep a daily or weekly "gratitude" journal in which you jot down what you are grateful for and why. The key is not to pressure yourself to write for a certain length each time or at a set frequency but rather to write when you feel moved or inspired to express yourself with words. It's best to consider journaling as a meaningful and positive activity — never a chore or requirement.

Of course, not everyone is inspired by or comfortable with keeping a journal. You may find that other creative endeavors allow you to express your inner thoughts and feelings in a healthy and positive way. For example, playing an instrument may be your preferred form of artistic expression and self-discovery. Others find art, crafting, and/or performance to be productive and inspirational outlets for self-expression. If you aren't sure how to express or tap into your creative side, consider looking into classes at your local community center, such as dance, choir, painting, or theater. Some high schools offer courses and/or clubs in these areas as well. You may be surprised by your creative talents in addition to finding unique and rewarding passions for self-expression.

No matter what forms of creativity you choose, it's important to discover, pursue, and nurture them as a teen. This will not only give you the chance to explore who you are and what makes you feel fulfilled, but it will also provide a healthy balance between all the other tasks and commitments that come along with the teen years. In addition, you may find a welcoming community of people who enjoy the same creative outlets. Overall, recognizing and embracing the power of self-expression, whether through journaling or other forms of creativity, will enhance your personal growth as well as your lifelong journey of health and happiness.

# DOWNTIME AND RELAXATION

As this book has covered, self-care is essential for your overall health and wellness. In addition to staying hydrated, eating healthy, participating in physical activity, and getting enough sleep, allowing yourself periods of downtime and relaxation each day is also beneficial and important to your well-being. Teens often feel pressured to be doing something at all times, whether it's studying, socializing, or participating in activities. However, regular intervals of personal peace and quiet can reduce stress, frustration, fatigue, and even physical pain. In addition, when you allow yourself some downtime each day, you can improve your concentration, quality of sleep, and immune health.

Of course, everyone has a different concept of downtime and what it means to relax. Most experts consider relaxation to be a physical, emotional, and mental state in which someone experiences little to no tension or stress. There are formal techniques that you can learn to help relax your breathing, muscles, and even your mind and thoughts, such as yoga, meditation, and other mindfulness exercises. Some people enjoy walking, running, swimming, and other physical activities as ways to reduce tension and clear their minds. Others might prefer more quiet or restful forms of relaxation, such as reading, journaling, crafting, or just daydreaming. You may find that different types of downtime work for you depending on your daily schedule and how you're feeling. Ultimately, the goal is to set aside an intentional amount of time each day for an activity that doesn't require any specific focus or attention, providing you with a sense of rest and renewal.

When you are busy with school, work, sports, extracurriculars, and other commitments, it might feel wrong or even selfish to take some downtime. However, scheduling regular breaks for your mind and body can actually increase your productivity, creativity, time management, and critical thinking. Periods of calmness allow your body and brain to recover and recharge, which helps to restore physical and mental health as well. Therefore, daily intervals of downtime are fully in your best interest as a healthy, happy, and productive individual. Even if your days seem completely structured and full, giving yourself a few moments of relaxation, at least in the morning and evening, can be extremely beneficial for your overall wellness.

Many people consider scrolling through social media or casual online searching to be relaxing. Though this may feel like a leisurely activity, mindless or "doom" scrolling can negatively impact your well-being by interfering with sleep and increasing anxiety. In fact, any use of digital screens has the opposite effect of relaxation on your brain. Experts have found that screen time overstimulates our senses, fragments our attention, and drains our mental and emotional capacity. So, rather than feeling recharged and renewed after interacting with our digital devices, it's much more likely that we feel enhanced frustration, isolation, fogginess, and stress—whether we realize it or not. Knowing this, it's important to regulate and limit your screen time and do not consider turning to any digital devices to relax.

As a teen girl, it can feel difficult and overwhelming at times to prioritize your self-care. It may also feel strange at first to intentionally take quiet moments to reflect and just be present with your own thoughts and feelings. However, the more you consciously allow yourself to relax and experience true downtime, the more familiar and enjoyable it will become. The teen years hold the opportunity for you to discover who you are, develop lifelong healthy habits, and grow as a person. The best way to do this is to take good care of yourself by achieving a balance between what you must do and what makes you feel both passionate and at peace.

# CHAPTER TWELVE:
# LIFE SKILLS AND
# PRACTICAL KNOWLEDGE

To some teens, it can seem as if adults just inherently understand how to navigate the world. The adults you know may even give the impression that having a career, raising a family, running a household, and taking care of problems as they arise all come naturally and rather easily. Of course, this is a false impression. What many call "adulting," or successfully living as an adult, is the result of years spent acquiring life skills and practical knowledge. It certainly doesn't happen all at once, and these learning experiences usually continue throughout a person's life. Imagine all the adults who had to learn how to transition from basic landline phones at home to the nearly unlimited capabilities of carrying personal cell phones!

Therefore, it's never too early to start gathering the basic skills and knowledge that will assist and benefit you as you grow into adulthood. This would include such principles as learning how to manage your time, money, and personal health. It's also important to develop interpersonal skills, such as effective communication and relationship building, to help you navigate social and professional settings. Other basics that are beneficial as you grow and mature are organizational skills, critical thinking, self-motivation, decision-making, and developing coping strategies to build resilience.

Most pre-adults learn a great deal from observing their environment, the way people function, and how things work. Parents, siblings, older family members, neighbors, and friends may also model helpful skills and/or teach them to you directly. For example, you may have practice driving sessions with your mother when you get your learner's permit, and she may also teach you how to put gas in the car or check the air pressure in the tires. There are likely to be numerous resources available, in person and online, to teach you all types of skills and present helpful knowledge that you can carry into your future. But keep in mind that you also have plenty of time to learn what you'll need to navigate adulthood, so there is no reason to feel pressured to figure out everything immediately.

Building life skills and gaining practical knowledge are important to becoming self-sufficient as an adult. Self-sufficiency is when you have the ability to take care of yourself and provide for your needs to achieve basic independence. For example, you might already be self-sufficient in getting yourself up and ready for school each day by setting an alarm, eating breakfast, getting dressed, gathering your backpack, and leaving on time without being reminded of all these steps. However, being self-sufficient doesn't mean that you won't require occasional help or support; instead, it reflects a person's resourcefulness, competence, and sense of responsibility, in addition to recognizing when assistance is needed.

Ultimately, you are accumulating life skills and practical knowledge every day through observation, experience, asking questions, and even trial and error. If you find yourself particularly interested in building a certain life skill or wish to gain more practical knowledge about something, don't hesitate to set those goals and find the resources to pursue and achieve them. For instance, you may want to understand more about starting an herb or vegetable garden when you eventually have your own space. Or you may want to enhance your knowledge of geography in case you have opportunities later in life to travel. Even if you don't end up having direct use for these competencies or proficiencies in adulthood, the learning process is valuable in itself and will help you better navigate your future path.

# BASIC DAILY
# TASKS

Many teens live with one or more parents/adults who generally take care of running most of the household. This can include shopping for groceries, cooking, cleaning, doing the laundry, home and vehicle maintenance, and more. Though everyone's contribution to their household community and chores may be different, it's important as a teen girl to learn basic survival skills so that you can be self-sufficient when the time comes. This isn't limited to domestic activities like cooking and cleaning, but learning those skills is a good way to start building your independence and benefiting your future.

Cooking skills may seem outdated for some people with today's readiness of prepared meals and the ease of ordering food deliveries. However, learning to cook offers you the chance to explore different foods and types of cuisine in addition to ways of preparing them. In most cases, cooking for yourself is more cost-effective and healthier as well — even if you are just able to make basic meals for breakfast, lunch, and dinner. In addition, as you explore the world of cooking, you may learn that you have undiscovered culinary talents and passions.

There are many options when it comes to learning cooking skills. For example, if you have family members who are good cooks, you can ask them for lessons. This is a great way to make meaningful memories as well as learn family recipes and history. There are also numerous food networks and online tutorials, including recipes and videos, for learning how to cook just about anything. You may also find time to check out cookbooks that teach the basics from your local library or even take a cooking class at a nearby community center. Ultimately, learning to cook is an important life skill that can enhance both your health and happiness in addition to furthering your independence and self-sufficiency.

Cleaning is another important skill to learn as a teenager. There is a good chance that you, like most teen girls, are asked to clean and tidy up your bedroom periodically in addition to other chores such as taking care of the dishes, laundry, bathroom, or vacuuming. Though cleaning may not necessarily bring out the same passion and creativity as cooking for most people, it is beneficial for your health and well-being in many ways. Of course, keeping a sanitary and well-maintained environment is important for your physical wellness and safety. In addition, completing cleaning and organizing tasks can also reduce your stress, anxiety, and tendency to procrastinate. For example, if you come home from a long day to a chaotic or unclean environment, you are likely to feel a sense of unease or unhappiness rather than comfort and peace. In turn, this may affect your mental health and ability to focus.

Poor cleanliness habits may also negatively impact your future relationships with college roommates, officemates, romantic partners, etc. Nobody is expected to be perfect; if you occasionally don't make your bed, that's not a character flaw. However, basic cleaning skills are easy to learn, and they will have long-term benefits for your health and wellness, your relationships, and your environment. If you are uncertain about what to clean or how to do it, there are many online checklists and tutorials to consult for help. The basics would include putting items where they go, tossing out garbage, wiping counters, vacuuming and/or mopping floors, washing dishes and linens (such as sheets and towels), and dusting furniture and surfaces. Remember that you don't have to strive for perfection—just a relatively clean and organized space.

There are many basic skills to build on your journey to being self-sufficient, but keep in mind that you aren't expected to learn them all at once. In the meantime, you can practice good strategies in self-sufficiency by observing capable and successful adults around you; being accountable for your time, space, and actions; and gaining as much practical experience as possible. Taking opportunities to be responsible for yourself as you grow will increase your self-confidence, skills, and knowledge so that you will be prepared to embrace independence when the time comes.

# PERSONAL SAFETY: ONLINE AND OFFLINE

Perhaps the most important commitment you can make as a teen girl is to keep yourself safe. Safety comes in many forms, from literal physical protection against harm to security against anonymous cyberbullies. Of course, accidents and unfortunate things happen to everyone. But when you are aware of and protect your personal safety, online and offline, you are much more likely to remain healthy and happy on your journey toward a successful future. In addition, you'll have a greater chance of avoiding outcomes that might adversely affect your life, both now and later.

Due to physiological and other factors, teens are more likely to engage in risky behaviors than other age groups. Such tendencies toward risk are a concern on their own in terms of personal safety, but this is often compounded by the fact that many teens don't have the foresight or understanding of potential negative and long-term consequences. For example, you might think underage drinking is harmless when you're with friends or at a party. Yet this behavior can result in significant and lifelong consequences, from physical harm to legal troubles and more. This applies to your digital life as well, including any participation in online discussions, posts, videos, or other content. What may appear innocent to you at the time might end up being taken out of context or difficult to explain much later when the stakes are higher, such as job interviews or college admissions.

Protecting your personal safety, whether online or offline, doesn't mean that you must behave perfectly with no mistakes or avoid taking healthy risks. An important part of growing up, in fact, is having different experiences, being spontaneous, and learning new things. Instead, personal safety requires an extra step when making decisions that many teens forget to take—and that is to think critically. Critical thinking is the ability to analyze and evaluate a situation through logic and reason rather than emotion and instinct. No matter the circumstances, where you are, or who you are with, you have the right (and responsibility) to take a moment and think critically about any potential harm or negative consequences before you act. There is no experience or person that is worth compromising your current and future integrity, health, and overall personal safety.

This leads to the most important lesson of all: *Your life belongs to you.* You have the right to say no. You have the right to change your mind. You have the right to protect your physical, emotional, and mental health. You have the right to be honest, safe, and to get help when you need it. You have the right to make decisions and choices when it comes to your heart, mind, and body. You have the right to determine who you are as an individual and to pursue your dreams and goals. You have the right to speak your mind, defend your values, and assert yourself as a person.

If you find that anyone is infringing on these rights or trying to compromise or violate your personal safety in any way, get help immediately from a trusted adult or proper authority. Your safety, security, and protection as a person should never be jeopardized by anyone, including yourself. Therefore, treat yourself as you would something precious, valuable, and irreplaceable.

# NAVIGATING
# THE WORLD

For the most part, being a teen girl is a positive experience and a time for self-discovery, personal growth, and joy. However, you may get the impression from society, media, or even close family members that young women are supposed to be nice and polite in ways that other groups are not expected to be. Though this mindset is antiquated and will hopefully evolve to achieve and reflect true equality and equity, there is still pressure to conform and to be agreeable or nonproblematic simply because you are a teen girl. It is important to resist these stereotypical limitations and remain strong in following your dreams and pursuing your goals. The only thing required and expected of you as a teen girl is what should be required and expected of all people—to treat yourself and others with integrity, compassion, and respect.

Thankfully, as you navigate the world as a young woman, there are many resources and ways to get support. Forming personal and professional relationships with other women from diverse backgrounds is an excellent way to learn from and bond with others. Be inquisitive with your mentors, teachers, coaches, community leaders, and family members so that you can get advice, have a greater understanding of their experiences, and apply it to your own journey. There are many women (famous and not-so-famous) that you can research as well to find sources of inspiration, originality, creativity, and more. Consider reading biographies and/or memoirs of women who have created new paths and made a difference for others. Reach out to your counselors and advisors for guidance and practical advice for your future.

Overall, it's important to keep in mind that you are not alone in navigating the world as a young woman. Though you are unique in terms of your individuality, ideas, talents, and passions, you share the experience of being a teen girl and growing into a woman with many people who can provide empathy, support, and knowledge. And soon, you will be able to do the same for others to continue that special legacy.

# CONCLUSION

No matter who you are or where you come from, the teenage years are certain to be as challenging as they are rewarding. This is especially true for today's teen girls, who face both unprecedented pressures and incredible opportunities as young women. The transition from girlhood to womanhood is filled with complex changes, exciting milestones, and hard work. That's why this handbook is a good resource when you need reassurance and encouragement.

At times, being a teenager can feel overwhelming, confusing, and even isolating. There are external pressures to succeed in all areas and conform to certain standards based on the expectations of society, peers, the media, and even family members. Teen girls also experience internal pressures and expectations for themselves as they plan for the future and work toward their dreams. One of the goals of this book is to ensure that you understand that you are not alone when it comes to your thoughts, emotions, and even changes in your body. In addition to offering comfort and solidarity, another goal of this handbook is to promote self-care and help you prioritize your physical, mental, and emotional health. This is one of the most important keys to reaching your highest potential, fulfillment, and empowerment.

Above all, the purpose of this book is to convey and reinforce the message that you are not limited by being a young woman but rather that this is exactly what makes you strong, unique, and capable of achieving amazing things. You are entitled to assert personal boundaries, be your true self, and take advantage of all the opportunities that come your way. Your passions, interests, and goals are an important part of your identity and path to success, and you deserve to freely pursue them as a means of self-actualization. Of course, you will have commitments, responsibilities, and relationships that will require your attention and time as a teenager and beyond. But overall, you are in charge of your choices, actions, and the many other aspects that determine who you want to be and what you wish to do—now and in the future.

Keep in mind that no handbook is large or detailed enough to cover everything that a teen girl is likely to experience, and your journey will differ from everyone else's in many ways. The good news is that there are many sources of support, including this book, to help you navigate the exciting and transformative times of teenage girlhood. As you progress through school, relationships, activities, events, and more, it's important to remember that there will be significant accomplishments and joys but also challenges along the way. Therefore, staying authentic and true to your values is essential as a means of keeping you centered. Resilience is also key for overcoming adverse circumstances and situations when and if they present themselves. Ultimately, your path as a teen girl will be one of self-discovery as you gain the tools and knowledge to become a self-actualized and successful adult with each step you take.

Made in the USA
Coppell, TX
16 November 2024

39987547R20079